WITHIN THE ASHES

CIN MEDLEY

MED'S PUB

Within
the
Ashes

CIN MEDLEY

Published by: Med's Pub Publishing
Copyright © 2018 Cin Medley
All Rights Reserved
ISBN-13: 978-0-9989748-3-5
ISBN-10: 0998974838
Cover Design: Amanda Walker Design Services
Edited by: Kendra's Editing and Book Services
Formatted by: Med's Pub Publishing

My undying gratitude

My husband and my daughter, who put up with my crazy thoughts, and singing. I love you both.

Amanda Walker, who is so talented and a new friend, who makes all the pretties, thank you for invading my world and making yourself known.

Michelle Windsor, my friend and fellow author. I am grateful that you helped me come out of my closet and encouraged me to be known. You make me smile.

To my readers, who make me want to write. I can't thank you enough.

To the faithful readers of Becca Storm:

Even though it is very unusual to do something like this, I believe this to be a most unusual manuscript.

My name is Paula Emerson. I was once married to a man named Alexander Railing and was a publisher for Railing Publishing. I had the honor of publishing Becca Storm's first book, then her second, third, and now her final book, this one.

I was party to a portion of the truth that lies between these pages but not to any of the real deceit. I knew who my husband was, and yes, I married the man, so I could enjoy the lifestyle his family's wealth afforded me.

But I also cheated on him. He was not a great lover; in fact, he was… well, he sucked in bed. I broke my pre-nup, and when the fiasco of a marriage came to an end, I was left with nothing. No job, no home, nothing.

Becca made a deal with the fucking devil to make sure I was taken care of. I know, at the time, she didn't realize what she was doing. I thank you for that.

I received this manuscript a few months ago, and I've been holding on to it. I've read it over at least ten times, and each time my heart is torn in two. I am not only honored to know her, but I am humbled by the fact that she even considered me.

She wrote me a letter, which I have enclosed at the end of this book, and made me promise to not change a thing, and I haven't.

I suppose, what I want to say is that no matter what happens in our world, in our life, there is always something waiting for us.

Thank you, and now, I give you the very final Becca Storm manuscript.

Sincerely,

Paula Emerson.

CHAPTER ONE

I haven't touched a computer in nearly eight months, but both my agent and publisher are holding me to my contract to produce yet another best seller. But how can a best-selling writer write a book when the stories have ended, when that writer's life has ended?

Janet, my agent, tells me to just put my fingers on the keyboard and the story will come.

Well, I'm sitting here, Janet, and I've got nothing.

My publisher sweetly reminds me through Janet that I have a contract. Everyone is understanding, considering. I shake my head at the word.

Considering.

What kind of word is that anyway? Considering. I know what it means, even what it should mean. But why do we use it? It's used as an excuse, basically, for not doing something, or for excusing someone's behavior.

What's wrong with just saying the truth? I have nothing left inside of me to write. No words will come. That's the truth; that's my truth.

My mind is blank, Janet.

My pages are empty, Paula.

The ride of my life is done, gone, blown to the wind in nothing but ash.

CHAPTER TWO

So, another month has passed, and I am still here, separated from the world on what most days feels like the end of the earth. I walk along the beach that surrounds this lake I've managed to escape to, but I rarely see anyone. I go into town once a month to get the things I need to survive.

The little car I bought when I arrived nine months ago still has less than a hundred miles on it. I have nowhere to drive. The world has nothing left for me anymore. All that I love is just gone. Gone in the night, in the blink of an eye.

As I turn my head, I can see the only thing of them I have left. The tiny, folding, wooden picture frame that holds their pictures sits on the bookcase underneath the wall of windows overlooking the lake. My tablet is filled with recorded videos of conversations we've had, videos that I can't bring myself to watch. Closing my eyes, I want to believe that they felt nothing. I tell myself that God was graceful enough to make it quick and painless. According to the authorities, there was no time for anything. They were all still sleeping, the dog still curled up near my husband's feet at the foot of the bed.

That's how fast it all happened. That's how fast my life ended.

I spend most days trying to figure out why I wasn't home. I mean, I know why I wasn't home, but why was I left here to suffer and to feel? The pain sears through me and cuts away any kind of warmth that might normally flow through my veins. I'm cold. I'm unfeeling to anything, to anyone. Most days, I sit on the deck and drink my tea, looking at the calm waters of the lake outside my door.

The sun rises each morning and sets each night, but I am just existing. I've thought about joining them, but I think about how pissed off John would be. He was the one who encouraged me to write. When I quit my job when our son was born, he told me I was a fantastic editor and that I should just do what I had been talking about doing since he met me.

I smile at the memory, because that's all I have are the memories. He came home from work one day with a huge computer.

"I bought you a present," he said as he came bouncing into the house.

His perfect smile flashes in my mind. He was so proud that he had went and picked it out all by himself. "So you can write the next Great American Novel."

We laughed about it all through dinner. But I had some great ideas. I was excited and happy that this man wanted me to pursue my dream of being a writer.

Yeah, well, I pursued them all right, right to the top of the New York Times Best Seller List. It shouldn't have happened like that. I should have paid my dues. But having friends in the business took me from a housewife and mother, to a name that everyone knew in a ridiculously short amount of time. Hell, I had people calling me to go on talk shows. I'm not that kind of person; I never was. I just wanted to write, to stay at home and watch my children grow.

By the time my first book was finished and rose to the top, I was pregnant with our second child.

I never wanted to be thrust into the bright lights of famedom—yes, Paula, I know it's not a word. All I ever wanted was to just tell the stories. So, I sat down between naps, breastfeeding, laundry, and taking care of my family and wrote my second book. When it hit the bookstores, our daughter was just shy of two years old and our son was four. It seemed as if it was an overnight success. That's when I met Janet.

My old boss, Sid, sent her my way. I didn't want an agent, but John thought I should have someone to help with all the publicity my books were getting. He thought I should go out and market myself. I think he secretly liked the idea that his wife was this famous writer.

Stupid man. If only they had come with me. But, he thought I should go to New York by myself, that I should have some time away from him and the kids. I didn't want to go. I hated to be away from them.

~

I needed to stop. A few weeks have passed now. It's been nearly ten months, and I still can't breathe.

Paula, I hate you right now.

Janet, I know your advice makes sense, to just put my fingers on the keyboard and let the words come.

I'm afraid this reads like the worst book ever written. So, I'm taking a deep breath. I've told myself that I will continue with what seems to be my story. The beginning to the end of all that I hold dear. The beginning to the end of who I am as a woman, as a person, as a human being.

So, Janet pretty much did nothing for the first year or so of her employment. I think back at how persistent she was, trying at every turn to get my name out in the world of literature.

It's not what I wanted. It's not who I am. It wasn't until my third book that John pushed me.

"Bec, you obviously have a beautiful talent, a way with words, so much so that people want to hear what you have to say. They want to see you, to get to know you. At least, consider it."

See, there is that word again. Consider. This time, it was telling me to think carefully about something. The more I considered it, the more I thought about it, the more I knew it wasn't what I wanted to do. But then Janet called, telling me some Hollywood executive approached her about making my first book into a movie. He wanted to buy my book. My book. What the hell was that? How do you buy someone's book? Did it mean I'd need to give up the copyright? I wasn't so sure I could do that. It felt like someone asking me to buy my baby.

I mean, writing a book, putting your story on paper and then putting it out into the world for others to read, to ridicule, to dissect… It's like handing your child over to a group of strangers and then sitting back while they rip him apart. I couldn't do it. I couldn't let any of them go.

John convinced me, though. He said it would be the same as watching one of our children being honored, like watching them graduate high school. With his encouraging words, I agreed to a deal that allowed me to keep my copyright. I could keep my baby. That was when our life changed. I'm not so sure it was the best change. Money wasn't something we needed to worry about to begin with.

We had the winery John's family had owned forever. When his parents passed away, it was left to him. In fact, I met him there while on a wine tasting trip with a group of friends. He was so attentive to us, more so than he was to anyone else there. I think, at the time, he was with someone, because a woman kept coming over and touching his arm, trying to draw his attention away from us. But he refused to leave. By the end of our tour, he had asked me for my number.

"Would it seem odd to you if I asked for your number?"

I think I might have been a bit drunk because I giggled, but I glanced past him to the woman shooting daggers in my direction and asked, "Wouldn't your girlfriend be upset with you?"

He turned to follow my sight line. "She's not my girlfriend; although, she wants to be." He leaned in, adding, "She isn't really my type."

His response sent me into a giggle fest. "Well, I suppose I could give you my number." I remember I secretly wanted to shove it in her face. He waited a few days and then called me. I still can't believe I slept with him on our first date. He was so delicious, and man could he kiss. After that, we were inseparable, and four months later, we were married at the vineyard with only a few friends and our families.

For ten years, we were married; I suppose we still are. Until death do us part. I still twirl my rings around my finger, a habit I find myself doing more and more lately. In my heart, I am still married to him, so I haven't been able to bring myself to remove them. He is the love of my life; they all are. My heart, my soul, and now there is nothing but this void. A series of endless days and nights filled with silence. I can barely hear my children's voices anymore, their laughter. I can't feel his lips on mine or feel his body pressed against mine when we made love.

God, John, I miss you so much. How am I supposed to do this life without you?

It feels like a lifetime ago. For him, it was, because he no longer has a life. There is nothing remaining where our life was lived. Nothing but ash and bricks. I was left with a suitcase full of clothes that I will never wear again, my little wooden picture frame, my tablet full of memories I can't bring myself to watch, and our selfie on my phone which I haven't turned on the entire time I've been here.

As I continuously wipe tears from my cheeks, I move on through the days. In the beginning, every morning that I woke, it felt strange to roll over to an empty, cold bed, so I now sleep on the couch. I miss his smell. I miss the wet towels on the floor in the bathroom. I miss the cherished way only he could make me feel. I miss how he would get inventive in our bed late at night, how we would experiment, how he loved me.

God, it's all gone, all of it. Everything. I am nothing. I have nothing.

Fuck, Janet, you piss me off. I don't want to do this. I don't have anything left inside of me. I flat lined that night Hell blew through my life and ended it.

∿

I had to walk away from this damn computer again. I couldn't do it anymore.

Paula, I'm really sorry for the words on these pages.

Janet, I hate you for bringing this damn thing to me. I never should have told you where I was.

But I also have to thank you both for being my friends and for pushing me, however slowly, into facing what has become my life.

I lay on the beach for hours at a time, just waiting. Waiting for what, I'm not sure. Perhaps, I wait for a sea monster… well, a lake monster to drag itself up onto the sandy white shore and eat me. Like in the movie "Lake Placid", maybe a giant alligator lives in these calm waters. I just lay there with no thoughts, no feelings, nothing in my head. I do this every day, just as I have for the past ten months.

There is no story floating, no pretense of words that might form a story, or even the outline of a story. There is absolutely nothing. As I sit here and type on this retched machine, I am literally writing the thoughts as they come. I exist here. That is all. Nothing more. I breathe in and out all day, desperately hoping it's all a dream—a huge fucked-up dream—but it's not.

As I stood in a room with a hundred people and read my husband's favorite part of the book, I remember smiling, thinking about how much we laughed when I read it to him later in the night after our children went to bed, the day I wrote it. While I wanted nothing more than to look out and see his face in the crowd, a raging evil swept across the land and swallowed my life.

He was my strength in a crowd such as that. He never missed one reading. He was my calm before the storm of emotions that rumbled inside of me each and every time I stood in front of a microphone. I can close my eyes and still hear his voice on the phone before I left the hotel.

"Knock 'em dead, babe. You'll do fine, better than fine. You know how I know this?"

"No, how do you know?"

"Because you are the bravest, smartest woman I have ever known.

Do you really think I would have married a coward? You can do this, and when you're done, you will call me and tell me I was right."

Well, Janet, Paula, when I was done, I called him, only to hear that retched sound. That sound still echoes in my mind, invades my thoughts. That sound meant it was over. My fairy tale, my happily ever after was gone. That sound will forever mark the end of the stories. The end of me.

It's weird how I felt a chill that night, even though it was only early fall in the city. I knew somewhere deep inside that something was terribly wrong. I didn't even greet the people right after. I moved to the back of the stage and dialed my phone, praying that chill was just caused by the lack of heat, but it wasn't. There were too many people in the room, too many people breathing and exhaling for a cool draft to wash over me.

Remember, Janet? Remember the way I started to hyperventilate? Remember how I demanded to go to the airport immediately? Remember when the driver was talking about how the fires in California were out of control? Remember running through the airport with me, to find a television to see the news? Remember my screams when I heard that Napa had burned?

I remember. I remember it all like I am still living it. I am still living it. I live it every fucking day.

'Knock em dead, babe.' If I could have let everyone in that room die instead of them, instead of him, instead of my babies, I would have gladly traded them and then worried about my sins later. My heart is broken. My soul is dead. I am a walking dead person. My heart beats, but it beats for no one. It beats because my brain tells it to. It doesn't speed up for anything, but then again, I don't do anything but sit and drink tea with an empty mind.

I'm sorry, ladies, but I'm brain dead.

Dead, death, la muerte, décès... No matter what language you say it or write it, it all means the same thing: a permanent cessation of all vital functions, the end of life. This is me without them. This is them. *FUCK!* For the first few months, I kept asking God why He would do this to me. To them. Come on, nothing about this is right. NOTHING!

They say there are seven stages of grief: shock or disbelief, denial, bargaining, guilt, anger, depression, and acceptance or hope. So, let's see where I am.

Shock? Yep, still in shock. Denial? Nope, there is no denying this is real. I've never denied that my husband, the man of my heart, and my children, who my heart beat for, are gone.

So, what's next? Bargaining. I laugh at this one. How can you bargain with the forces of evil itself? Fire. There is no bargaining with that shit. One minute, you are there, asleep in your bed, and the next, you are breathing in toxic fumes that ultimately take that very breath away. Then your body burns, and burns, until there is nothing left but bone and ash, where once was warmth and love and life. So, I didn't bargain.

Next, we have guilt. Oh, you can bet your sweet ass that I have guilt. So much guilt that I could build a staircase to the fucking sun with guilt. I'm guilty of living a life outside the one I promised my husband I would live with him. A life together, for better or worse, in sickness and in health, 'til death do us part. Yep, death. It's one of those words, like considering.

So, next, we have anger. I laugh at this one. I will always be angry. It will never end, this anger that rages inside of me. It courses through my veins like a fucking run-away train. It will never end, it will never mellow, and it will never be done.

After anger comes depression. I'm not depressed; I am broken. My heart is broken, and my soul is empty. This vessel that I use to breath is empty. I feel like a flower bed with no flowers. A barren tree in the winter, only when spring comes nothing grows. It's not dead. It's dormant. That's what I am—a broken, hollow, dormant tree.

So, the next step is acceptance or hope. Acceptance of what? The fact that I have nothing? The fact that they are gone? That I will never smell my children again, or touch them? That my husband's hands will never caress my body? His lips will NEVER touch mine again. I don't, won't, and will never accept that. It's ridiculous to think anyone could accept that. And hope, what the fuck would I have hope for? Hope that the mysterious creature I pray lives in this calm lake will eat me one day? Hope that I die sitting in the fucking chair drinking my tea? Hope that what, one day I can be happy again? Absolutely ridiculous. Absofuckingridiclous.

CHAPTER THREE

It's been weeks since my last rant. I apologize. It's not like I am sitting here feeling sorry for myself. I've never had the 'poor me' type of personality. But you want me to write a book that I am contracted for, and I kept telling you that I have nothing to write. You said seventy-five thousand words, no less. Well, so far, we are close to thirty-two hundred. So, I suppose, I have seventy-two thousand more to go.

I met a dog on the beach today, a sweet black and white Border Collie. She just came over and laid down next to me. It was kind of comical really. She didn't say much, just licked my hand and then laid her head down on her paws. She sat with me for maybe an hour. I'm not sure; I've no conception of time anymore. I couldn't even tell you what day of the week it is, or what the date is. But she eventually got up and moseyed down the beach and then disappeared into the tall grass.

To be honest, it felt nice. I should be careful. It's been eleven months and I had a feeling. I wonder what that means? Maybe I should look into getting a dog. No, I couldn't replace Sadie. I don't want anything that can be taken away from me, not now, not ever again.

I think, no believe, that when you suffer such a loss, perhaps, there is no coming back from that. I don't think I have spoken to another person since Janet dropped this horrible machine off to me. To be honest, I don't mind. I don't mind at all.

So, where did we leave off? Oh, yes, the seven stages of grief. It's perfectly clear to me that I am still living in several stages of grief. Five of them, and it's been nearly a year. A year. One year. Three hundred and sixty-five days. Is it less? No fucking way. The pain still stops me from feeling. I can't do this.

Animals are weird. I used to say that about Sadie. She would always know when the mailman was coming. She hated him. Can dogs tell time? I was sitting on the beach earlier. Get used to it. I sit there every fucking day, waiting for the lake monster to emerge and take me to my family. It never happens. Do you think I'm crazy yet?

Anyway, I was sitting there with my cup of tea, my feet buried in the sand, complete and utter silence. The sound of the water lapped gently on the shore, and out of nowhere, with absolutely zero sound, here came this dog. She just wandered over and sat down next to me, looked me in the face, and then turned her head and looked out at the water. I wonder if she knows of the lake monster.

She just sat there with me; again, not a big talker. I didn't want to pet her, or talk to her, and I didn't ask her name. We just sat there. Then, I suppose when she was done with her thoughts, or prayers, or whatever, she looked at me and got up and walked down the beach, disappearing into the tall grass. I can't help but wonder who she belongs to. There are only two other houses on this part of the lake, and as far as I know, no one has stayed in them in years. At least, that's what the real estate agent told me. So, I guess she is a mystery.

My mundane life of sleeping on the couch and drinking tea. I think I've lost weight. I only eat because my body makes me. I don't exercise; well, I guess walking on the beach is some sort of it, but I don't walk far. It's to the same spot every day. You can see my foot-prints in the sand, and you can see the imprint my ass makes. There are two indentions where my feet push into the sand. That's it. When it's cold, I sit on the chair wrapped in a blanket on the deck.

I don't have any more thoughts. Today is yet another blank day.

Well, another few days, maybe even a week have passed. It would seem that I've made a friend. Every day, she has come to sit with me or to lie with me in the sand. Today, I said hello to her. She smiled; at least, I want to think she smiled at me. I know it sounds crazy. Perhaps I am going crazy, but today, I was a bit excited to see her. I actually hoped she would come. It's weird to say that it was nice.

I sat there waiting for the lake monster to come, but he sure is taking his sweet time. Maybe he's waiting for the perfect opportunity to take me. I wish. While I sat there, she came over and sat down. Looking at her, I smiled. "Hey," I said. "I was wondering if you had a name?"

The dog looked at me, and her eyes didn't move as she stared into my soul. I think I might have lost my breath.

"My name is Becca, in case you were wondering."

I don't think she was, because she sighed and laid down, a bit closer to me than she usually does, so maybe it did matter to her that I formally introduced myself. We sat there for a very long time, and then she just got up and walked down the beach, and yes, again, she disappeared into the tall grass. I just laid on my back and looked to the sky.

I'm not sure why I do this, why I wait to see God. Why I want the heavens to open up and let me see them, let me know they are at peace, but I do. Every damn day I do, and every damn day I am disappointed. Every damn day, there is nothing. It's always nothing, but that is what my life is. Nothing.

Sitting here at this machine, looking at the words I have written, I realize that, after a year without them, I am still such a mess.

Sorry, Paula, that I missed my deadline.

Sorry, Janet, that I am such a horrible client.

Well, I'm back, not because I have anything really to say, but just in case. As I sat on my deck with my cup of tea, staring at the water, and looking at the sky, I heard some splashing where there shouldn't have been. To be honest, I was hoping it was the lake monster coming ashore to scout me out. But it was dark, so I couldn't really see anything.

What I could see wasn't a monster. It looked like a person walking in the water just shy of the beach. It made me wonder how often this person walks past my house. How many nights? Every night? To be honest, I panicked a little bit. But it wasn't until I heard more splashing that I realized it was her. I slowly got up and moved into the house, thankful that I didn't have any lights on, and I sat down here to let whoever reads this know that there is someone who walks the beachfront past my house. Just in case I get my wish, I want you to know that I am happy to be gone, happy to be with them.

Well, more days have passed and I'm still here. The stranger who walks the beach at night has been by once. It seems that it is an every-other-night occurrence, so I've made it a point to not sit on the deck on the nights that they walk. I still see my friend the Border Collie every day. Hell, today, she was waiting for me. Still, she is silent.

"So, do you come here often?" I asked her. I smiled when I said it. I swear, if she speaks to me, I think I might die right there. "I get it. Silence. You like to keep the mystery going. I can understand that," I said. It's strange to hear my own voice. I think, in the thirteen months that I've been here, those are the most words I've said. I don't mind. I really don't have anything to say.

Mostly, we just sit in silence until she gets up and walks down the beach to disappear into the tall grass. I've thought about following her just to see where it is that she goes, but yeah, I kind of like the mystery. I would be horrified if someone followed me home.

I've been doing some soul searching, thinking about this emptiness that now resides inside of me. I know I can never write like I did in the past. It's because of the writing that my life is over now. I think that's why the words have stopped. I know I won't ever write more than what you will read here. To be honest, as I've said before, these words exist only because I am bound by a contract to produce one more book. Seventy-five thousand words.

I'm sorry Paula, but this is the end.

I'm sorry Janet, but your employment with me has come to an end. When I turn this over, I'm out. I was out the night of the reading in New York. I'm pretty sure I could disengage our agreement with lawyers, but then I would have to interact with people, and I would have to give my reasons.

Paula, I would like to believe that you wouldn't sue me, and I know you believe that this book will make us both richer than we are, but it won't. I am just filling a quota here, a requirement.

I haven't read what I have written, and I don't want to read it. I just want to live in my lonely, empty world and wait for the day that I can be with them. I miss them so much. I finally opened my little wooden picture frame only to slam it shut. I can't bear to look at their faces. I can't deal with not knowing them anymore or wondering what kind of people they are turning into. Nothing pacifies this raw emptiness.

The days may be moving on, but my routine stays the same. I exist. I open my eyes every morning with nothing but regret and pain. I sit on my deck, drink my tea, and feel nothing. I think of nothing. I go and sit on the beach, and my friend the Border Collie comes and sits with me each and every day. I wonder what her owner must think, or if she even has an owner. She doesn't look like she is starving. Her coat is shiny, and her paws, from what I can see, aren't torn up. So, I just accept that this is what it is.

I think she feels that I might need her. To be honest, I am used to her. I think, if she didn't show up, I might even miss her. But I'm not going to tell her that. She might really think I'm needy then.

I went to the store today and thought about buying her a treat, or a bone, but then I thought how I'd feel if she was my Sadie. I would have got pissed if someone did that with her, so I put the treats back.

It's the night that the stranger walks, and I almost want to sit outside and see if I can see who it is. I know it's the Border Collie's owner, but if they see me, as well, that would mean I would need to engage, and well, yeah, that's not on my list of things I want to do. So, I will just sit in the dark living room and drink my tea. It's nice not having anyone around.

~

Well, I saw him today, and yes, it's a him. He walked out onto the beach looking for her. I know he is her owner because her ears shot up and she jumped up and ran down the beach. I did notice, though, that she paused about halfway there to look back at me. It felt like she was making sure I was all right with her leaving me. I gave her a slight nod, and she turned and ran to him.

He stood there watching her, watching me. I turned my head back to the lake and finished my afternoon routine of sitting, staring off into the water with nothing on my mind. Well, that's not true; these pages are on my mind. I just want to finish this and be done with it. I want out. I want out of this mundane life. I want to go home to John and my sweet babies. But I suppose God has other plans for me. I just wish He would hurry the hell up.

~

The days go by, one after the other, minute by minute, hour by hour, and still there is nothing. I've just left my fridge, and it looks like I am off to the store. I am becoming tired of this writing of words that are just as dull as anything else. I just checked the word count. Hell, I only need seventy thousand more.

Aren't you just thrilled, Paula? I'm sure, soon, you are going to throw this manuscript across the room and yell, "Fuck!" I know I would.

Be back later, ladies.

Well, I'm back, and I think I might have something to say. I know you are waiting for something, anything that is going to resemble another best seller, but I'm sorry to say that isn't going to happen.

So, I went to the little store here in this semi-small town that services this part of the country. I suppose it's bigger then semi-small, but it's not a place where you would ever have to worry about getting caught up in a traffic jam. Hell, there are two stop signs. Yes, I go when I know I don't stand a chance in hell of seeing anyone, especially children. I haven't laid eyes on one since I kissed mine goodbye at the airport in Napa.

But that's not the reason for this little jaunt across the keys. So, I was in the store and decided that, perhaps, I should cook something, some meat. I stood at the butcher's looking at the selection of meat before deciding on a pork chop, a few ribs, and a very small steak. While he wrapped everything up, I suddenly got the feeling that I was being watched. I didn't want to turn around and look; I don't want anyone to look at me. If I were to look back, it would imply that I was open for a conversation. Yeah, that is not going to happen. If I didn't need food to survive, or even if I knew how to hunt, I would never leave my little house on the shores of the calm lake that holds the imaginary monster I dream will come and eat me.

But, and there is always a but in situations such as this, I took my packages from the butcher and turned to place them in my shopping cart that was probably as old as the people who founded the place. When I did, I happened to catch someone standing about fifteen feet away from me, looking at vegetables. I needed vegetables, but I just couldn't bring myself to walk over there. So, I was turning my cart, and, trust me, I tried with all I am not to lift my head up, but I did.

Looking back at me was a pair of deeply broken, gut-wrenching, soulful green eyes that literally took my breath away.

I didn't smile. I didn't do anything but walk away in the opposite direction. Needless to say, I didn't get my vegetables. I walked up to the register, checked out, and came back here. So, now, I am going to eat my meat with nothing else. I think I might consider moving further inward, as far away from civilization as I can get. Maybe I'll learn how to hunt, how to trap, and become Grizzly fucking Adams.

Ladies, I can't do this. I can't breathe. I am so broken.

CHAPTER FOUR

I haven't left the house for, I think, two weeks. I haven't written here in two weeks, and that was the last day I went to the store. I've been on the couch. I didn't eat my meat, either. I feel as if a hole has been punched into my chest. Intermittently, those eyes have appeared in my mind where nothing else has been. I feel stripped bare, as if all the skin on my body has been removed and I am lying here completely exposed, and the pain is beyond that.

It's been fifteen months, and it still feels like it was yesterday. Why? Shouldn't the pain have somewhat subsided by now? I mean, what the hell do I know about loss such as this? I didn't feel this gutted when my parents passed away.

I managed to make it to the beach. It wasn't my usual time, so the Border Collie wasn't there today. It felt strange, after weeks of having her company, not to see her. I laid on the sand, closing my eyes. I just laid there, waiting… For what, I haven't a clue. I just wish I could float away and be no more. I seriously think I've fallen into some form of depression.

As I laid there, I got that feeling again of being watched. When I turned my head toward her path, I could barely make out someone standing on the beach looking out at the water, and then running toward me was her.

Not willing to move, I just watched her run. She was beautiful and a sight for my sore and tired eyes. She ran right up to me, her tailing wagging, and she actually licked my face.

"Hi, sorry I've been gone. I'll try not to disappear again," I said to her.

She laid down next to me, cuddling into my side. I brought my arm to rest on her back, my fingers running through her hair. Her coat was soft, so I think she is well taken care of. I heard a whistle, and her head popped up.

"Go, I'll see you again," I said.

I felt tears well up in my eyes as she jumped up and ran away. I don't even know why I was crying. But I laid there with tears running down the sides of my face. It was ridiculous. It is ridiculous that I was crying because she had to go home. She doesn't belong to me. No one does, not anymore.

I got up and came here to put more words on these pages. Now, I think I'm going to take a bath. A long hot bath.

There really isn't anything I want to write down today. I'm not even sure why I turned this damn machine on. If I'm telling the truth, I think it brings me company. I feel as if maybe I am telling someone how I feel. Therapy.

I had a lovely bath; well, as lovely as a bath can be without someone you love holding you. It used to be our thing.

"To be honest with you, Bec, I don't think I ever taken a bath with a woman. You would be the first." His voice echoes in my head.

"Well, then you are in for a treat. It's so relaxing to just lie in the water and feel the calm."

I remember sitting in the water, watching him undress. He was so beautiful, his body perfect and all mine. His cock grew harder as each piece of clothing hit the floor.

"Have you ever had sex in water?" I asked him.

"No, but I've come in the shower a few times." Smiling, he continued, "Well, more than a few times. Why, are we going to have sex in the tub?"

I remember laughing. "If you don't get that thing under control, we just might." I'd licked my lips. He had such a superior cock. It was perfect.

I need to go for a walk.

As I walked along the beach, I realized I was heading toward the place she disappears to. I didn't want to go there, so I turned around and, for the first time, headed in the opposite direction. I had never walked this way. The beach was rocky down there, but I figured what the hell.

I didn't make it very far. I'm afraid that I'm not as sure-footed as most. So, I turned back and just came here. Came back to the keyboard that, believe it or not, is bringing me a bit of peace. It's becoming a source of solace for me. I swore I would never become dependent on anything or anyone for my... what? I don't even have a word to put there. It certainly isn't happiness, or joy, or contentment. I am none of those things.

I am becoming calm after all this time. I am becoming calm.

I think, tomorrow, I am going to go to the store and get my vegetables and have some meat. Maybe, if I get a bit stronger physically, then I can attempt to walk the rocky beach.

So, goodbye, ladies. I shall write some more to reach my quota...

I got my vegetables. Exciting, I know. I went to the beach today, and yes, she came to sit with me.

"Do you have a name, little girl?" I asked her.

I swear she nodded to me, but again, she remained silent. I wonder why she comes here to sit with me. Maybe she knows I need someone. Maybe she can sense that I am beginning to feel the wearing of my soul from being in this fortress of solitude. I'm lonely but not in the sense that I am lonely. I'm forgetting the sounds of my children's voices. I can't remember what it felt like when my husband touched me. I can't feel his breath on my neck or my lips as he kissed me. My memories are fading, and I think I might lose my mind.

I'm going to sleep.

I stayed in bed for two days, wanting, hoping for my dreams to include them. But they didn't come. They never come. I know, as a writer, I have written dream scenes, but they aren't a reality. I can't and haven't dreamt of them. I am at a loss for words. How do you describe indescribable pain, indescribable sorrow? There just aren't words. I used to be good at writing emotions. I suppose that they now belong to me, and because of the fact that I have nothing in my mind, I can't.

Well, I went to sit on the beach again, but my friend didn't come and see me. I know it's the regular time. Maybe she was being like me, promising to show up but not. I feel as if I let her down. I looked down the beach thinking maybe I should go, maybe I should get up and walk down there. But I couldn't. Her owner is there.

Standing up, I dusted off my ass and started back to my house, when I heard her barking. I turned to see her running down the beach. I'd be lying if I said that my heart didn't beat a little faster at seeing her. I sat down and waited for her to run up to me, and she nearly knocked me over. To be honest, I was so shocked at how it felt to feel her love for me that I busted out laughing, and then the tears came. I can't be happy without them. I don't have that right. I immediately got up and took off running, just leaving her standing there, like she did something wrong. Like it was her fault.

I don't understand how I'm expected to do this. Fifteen months and I can't feel. But today I did feel. I felt comfort in a dog that belongs to someone else, to someone who stands on the beach and looks at the calm water of this lake. I wonder if he is waiting for the lake monster to come and get him. I wonder if she is torn between the two of us. It doesn't matter, I realize. It just doesn't matter.

The days have moved forward, but I stay on the porch now, punishing myself. She still comes and sits on the beach, watching me, waiting for me to come down, but I can't. I just can't. I refuse to allow myself anything but the basic essentials of life. I feed my body and that's it. I don't deserve to have happiness, not without them. They don't have it, so why should I get to keep on living, keep on having a life? This is my life. I will sit on this porch until I die.

As I sat there watching her, she lay with her head on her paws, just looking at me. I can only imagine what she was thinking. She probably thinks I'm pathetic. I could see that, because I am. Her ears perked up, her body jumped, and she took off running down the beach. I wonder now if she could read my mind. Yes, run away, I think. As I watched her run, I realized that she didn't go into the tall grass but continued down the beach.

So, I was still sitting on the porch when I heard her barking, and then I saw it. I saw the black smoke. I couldn't tell you how or why, but my cup hit the porch and broke into pieces, and the next thing I knew, I was running. My lungs burned as I pushed myself. Fire. Her human was there; otherwise, she wouldn't have been there on the beach. As I ran past the tall grass, the smoke was thick and heavy. I could hear her barking. There was some sort of hedge just after the tall grass, and as I cleared it, I heard the scream.

It was blood curdling, deep, and full of pain. I stopped in my tracks, trying to catch my breath. There was a huge fire on the other side of the hedge in the sand. It looked like furniture was piled up in it. Then, there was her owner. He was the man from the store. He was on his knees and had tears running down his face.

I just stood there looking at him. His eyes shifted and landed right on mine. He stared at me with some kind of venomous hatred. I took a step back and watched as he slowly stood. He was big, bigger than John; at least, he looked it from where I stood. He turned and stormed back into the house.

Me, well, I turned around and took off running back to my house. Back to the safety of the four walls of my cocoon I so carefully picked out to spend my last days on this planet. The one away from the real world. The one where I was guaranteed no interaction with people.

When my feet hit the deck, I stopped running. I opened the door, and here I sit hours later, writing on this stupid machine. Writing fucking words that mean nothing. I need to get the fuck out of here.

CHAPTER FIVE

It's been days since I moved off the couch. Someone has been here. I heard them knocking more than once, but I didn't get up either time. I didn't answer the door. I think the fire took more out of me than I even thought possible. To see the flames so big, my heart stopped. That's what happened to my life. Literally, up in flames. I'm not so sure that life is worth it anymore.

Well, you'll be happy to know that I'm still here. I took a shower and went to the store. I felt like something chocolate. When I got home, there was a note on my door from the Border Collie's owner. Apparently, his name is Rick. This is what it said.

I came by a few times, well, more than a few times, to apologize for scaring you. I know I did, because every time I came over your car was here, but this time it wasn't.

I've had a rough time, and I had a bit too much to drink the other day. I am sorry.

Rick

I mean, seriously, what the fuck is that? Why should I matter to him? I don't matter to anyone. Sorry, ladies, but honestly, it's been a year and a half, and I've heard nothing from either of you.

I know I told you, Janet, not to come back here, but still, I think if you fucking cared about me, you would have. I was just a paycheck for both of you. I could be dead for all you know, so I don't even know why I'm writing these fucking pages. That's a lie. I know why I am doing this. Because I have never not done what was expected of me. I signed my name on the god damn contract, and it is legally binding, so you will get your fucking pages, all seventy-five thousand words. To be honest, I hope you fucking choke on them.

So, the Rick person, my friend the Border Collie's owner, hopefully made himself feel better by apologizing to me. But what the fuck do I care? Who knows? Who cares? Certainly not me.

The air is turning a bit chilly, so the seasons are changing. Pretty soon, there will be no more beach sitting in shorts and bare feet. Soon, it will be sweats, hoodies, and my UGG boots. I can't help but wonder how many more winters I will see. This will be my second without them. My second winter without them. Life is not fair.

It's been about a week since I last sat here. I'm sorry for being so mean. I love you both. I just want this to be over. I have just over sixty-seven thousand words to go, so I suppose it's redundant to even think about it.

I've pulled out my two pairs of sweats and my hoodie. My suitcase is still in the closet. I haven't opened it since you brought it to me, Janet. I can't. It's filled with too many memories. I just closed the closet door and put it back in the darkness, back in the hole, where I belong.

After a trip into town to buy another cup, I went back out today to sit on the deck. It doesn't really matter anymore. When I turned my head from the calm lake, where I secretly will a lake creature to appear so I can make myself its next meal, she was coming down the beach in a full run. Quite a bit of a ways behind her was him, her owner, Rick.

Since I didn't want to talk to him, to even acknowledge him, I stood up to come in the house to hide on my couch. That couch has become my bed, because I can't stand waking up and not seeing him next to me. But my friend the Border Collie started barking when I went to come inside. It caused me to pause and look at her. She was nearly to my deck, which I thought odd because she has never come up here before. But, this time, she flew up the stairs and actually jumped on me. We've had very little contact in the months she's been sitting with me.

I had to smile at her. It took a few moments to move my hand to pet her. She had her paws wrapped around my hips, and she laid her head on my stomach.

"What? You are acting like you missed me or something," I said to her.

She whimpered and licked my hand.

As I picked my head up, I noticed that her owner, Rick, was a few feet from my deck. He looked me in the eyes. "I am so sorry. She just took off on me. I've been trying to keep her away, so not to bother you. But she wanted to come."

I stood there looking at him, not saying a word.

"Come on, Ella. Let's leave this lady alone."

I looked down at her. "So, your name is Ella?" I whispered. "Hi."

She nuzzled my hand. I picked my head up, and he was staring at me. When he moved toward the deck, I don't know why, but I shouted at him, "No!" He stopped.

I looked at the dog. "You need to go," I whispered to her.

She dropped on the deck and leaned against my legs. Then, just as she ran up the stairs, she walked down them. I looked at him and then turned and went in the house, closing and locking the door.

So, now, here I sit, thinking I am the rudest bitch on the planet. I don't want to talk to him, to have conversations. I don't want to explain my life to anyone. I will live with this emptiness and these feelings alone. To explain them would be to relive them, but I can't relive the searing, crippling pain that rips through me on a daily basis, not more than I already have to and not for some strange man. It's less intense as I put them here, but to hear myself say them out loud would only make them even more real.

I talk when it's necessary to speak to people. I don't want to know anyone anymore. Never will I ever give fate, or destiny, the opportunity to take from me again. The only thing I have left is my life, and trust me, I will give it up in a heartbeat. I want my family. I want my fucking family. I want this all to be a huge mistake. I want this to be the worst nightmare imaginable. But it's not. It's real. It's all so fucking real.

I haven't cried for a few months, but yesterday, I cried, and I screamed, and I cried some more. I know it's pointless, useless, because it is what it is. I can't fix it. I can't change it. It just is. But then, I finally pulled myself up off the couch and took a shower. I've decided that I need to go down there and apologize for being a bitch.

Don't even get any ideas, ladies. It isn't going to happen. Both of you know that I don't have a mean bone in my body; well, in the body I inhabited sixteen months ago, two winters ago.

Funny how I am measuring my life by the fucking seasons. I now understand the term 'fuck my life'.

So, I headed down the beach, only to be met by my Border Collie friend. I think I confused her when I kept walking. As I approached the hedge, I stopped, closed my eyes, and took a deep breath before I continued. I walked up the sand to his giant fire pit of ash, where I'm pretty sure he burnt everything in his house.

I made it to the door, where I nearly knocked but then decided against it. I really didn't want to talk to him. I didn't want him to think we were going to be friends. I mean, we kind of share a dog. I get all the benefits of having a dog without any of the responsibilities. Kind of shitty of me to walk away, but I did.

As my feet left his patio, I heard the door open.

"Hello," he said softly.

I just stood there, unable to turn around. "I just came to say I am sorry for yelling at you," I told him. Then I started walking. I had a feeling he wasn't going to let me go that easily, and sure enough, he was as predictable as most men, and he followed me onto the beach.

"We haven't been properly introduced. I'm Rick, and this is Ella. She thinks highly of you."

I admit it, I smiled. "Yeah, well, she never mentioned you," I said back to him.

He laughed. "Can I offer you a drink?"

"I don't drink." I know you bitches are laughing right now, but getting drunk with him is not going to happen.

"Like nothing? I have water, pop, whatever you would like." He was trying to be funny.

I took a deep breath and told him, "I don't want a drink. I just wanted to say I'm sorry for yelling at you. Nothing more." Then I said under my breath, which I wasn't really sure I said out loud, "It will forever be nothing."

Then I closed my eyes and walked back to my house. I didn't feel him walking toward me, so I relaxed a little. I was nearly home when I saw a car pull up in my driveway. As I got closer to the house, I saw that it was him. He actually drove over. He walked up to the porch and sat on my stairs. I sort of stopped and sat down in the sand, looking at him.

Why is he doing this? I thought. As I looked at him, I realized he is quite attractive, if you like that rugged mountain man look. His hair was a bit longer than it should have been, and he had some growth on his face, but what stood out the most were his eyes. They are a bluish-green color. Gentle, kind. He just sat there looking at me. Ella came up behind me and laid in the sand next to me, looking at us both.

I didn't attempt to touch her. That's not what our friendship is about. I didn't talk to her, either. My eyes stayed on him. He finally got up and started toward me. My first instinct was to get up and go in the house, but I didn't move. He stopped a few feet from me and just sat there.

Neither of us spoke, but we didn't look away. We just silently studied one another. Creepy, I know, but it wasn't. I could see a myriad of emotions in his eyes. The biggest one was pain. He was hurt just like me. I wondered why. After about, I don't know maybe an hour, I got up and walked to my house, leaving him sitting on the beach. He didn't follow me. A few minutes after I came in, I heard his car start and pull out of the driveway.

I can just imagine what he must think. But honestly, I don't fucking care what he thinks. I didn't ask him to come here. I didn't ask him to sit on the beach. I don't want him to come here, and I don't want him to sit on my beach. I don't want the lake monster to think he is a better meal than me. I haven't asked God for a thing since they left me. But I am considering asking him to make this guy named Rick leave me alone. I don't want to leave my fortress of solitude, my house of pain and suffering. No one ever said I had to talk to him. So, if he comes back, I will do as I did today and just stay silent.

Well, I hesitated to go out to sit on the deck today. The weather is changing fast. The chill in the air is definitely cold. I suppose that winter is here. Soon, sitting outside isn't going to be a thing I can do for a while. So, it's to the couch for me. I should be a bear and sleep this season away. I wish I could be Rip Van Winkle and go to sleep, to only wake a hundred years from now. I wonder if the pain would still be here. It's all around me. It never leaves me.

My friend the Border Collie came to sit on the deck with me again today. I guess I should actually call her Ella, seeing how that's her name. But, hey, she doesn't call me Becca, so would it be considered rude if I call her by her name?

After some time passed, I asked her, "So, where is your human?" She picked her head up and looked at me. "Not that I care," I added.

She laid her head back down, and that was the extent of our interaction. She's a quiet one, that's for sure. I'm getting used to her coming around. I wonder if I will miss her when it's too cold out for her to come all this way. I'm sure I will find out. After her allotted time, she got up and looked at me and then left. I nodded to her, just before she turned and headed down the stairs. I watched her all the way to the tall grass, and then I came in here to write my words on these damn pages.

Janet, I was wondering, was there ever a time in your life when everything went wrong? I've never experienced that personally, until that day in New York. This pain, this emptiness, this total annihilation of self-worth is not something I would wish on anyone.

Paula, I know this isn't what you wanted from me, and for that I am sorry. But, and there is always a but in situations like this. It's like consider, and death. It's a word we use to enter into an excuse. There is no excuse for this, for me. I just don't have it in me. It's been seventeen months, and no words have come. No story has evolved in my mind. I feel like that *American Pie* song by Don McLean. 'The day the music died', is part of the lyrics. April eighth is the day the words died. Nearly two years, Paula, and nothing. Just the stupid, shallow, wimpy words of a broken woman, a destroyed soul, a shattered heart.

Good night, I feel hibernation coming.

Well, this should get your feathers to ruffle. I couldn't tell you how much time has passed, but the ground is covered in snow. I haven't opened a curtain or the door.

I've slept mostly, cried a great deal, and ate only because my body is so weak. I have withered away to nothing. My clothes hang on me, but this is all irrelevant. I am going to keep my word and deliver to you my seventy-five thousand words, and then I am going to just disappear.

But today, I needed to go to the store. My body isn't going to survive on yogurt alone, so I broke down and showered and then headed out. When I walked out, my deck was cleared of snow, my chair was cleared of snow, a path had been shoveled to my car, and my car was cleared. I know it was her owner because I could see the paw prints in the snow. My drive was shoveled or plowed. Why didn't I hear this?

I'm not sure if I was grateful or pissed. I think, in the end, pissed was the emotion that was flying through my body. I made it to the store and packed my car with food, and as I was checking out, the cashier wished me a Merry Christmas. I was like, *what the fuck?* I stood there looking at her like she was insane.

She smiled. "It's Christmas Eve."

I nodded like I knew what the hell she was talking about. "Thank you. You have a lovely holiday," I said to her, pushing my very full cart out to my car.

What the fuck? Like I want to be reminded of this fucking day? I really need to get a fucking calendar so this doesn't happen again. I thought I had more time to isolate myself for this fucking holiday. Jesus Christ.

I had to be mindful of this rage pulsing through me on the drive back to my place. The roads were icy, and I didn't want to end up wrapped around a tree. Wait, is this me caring about what happens to me? Holy shit. Anyway, when I got home, there was this little box sitting on my porch in front of my door. It was wrapped with Christmas paper and even had a fucking bow on it.

Yep, you guess it. The son of a bitch gave me a fucking present. I mean, really? I brought in all my groceries and took the box and went to his house. There were a few cars in the driveway, but I really didn't take notice of them through the blind anger that was raging through me. It wasn't until I pulled up and nearly hit one of them that I saw them.

I got out, walked up to his front door, and rang his door bell. Who the fuck has a door bell in the middle of nowhere? He opened the door with a huge smile on his face. Yeah, well, it wasn't there when I left.

"Hi," he said. "Merry…" was all he got out.

"Did you leave this at my house?"

He nodded, still smiling. Like I should be fucking grateful that he gave me a present. I thrust it toward him.

"Please, don't leave things on my deck. You don't know me, and trust me when I tell you, you don't want to know me. I don't want to know you. Just stay away from me. I'm not someone you want to get close to. Believe me when I tell you I want nothing to do with you."

His smile left his face. "I bought that for you," he said softly. The look on his face was one of a child whose father ran over his puppy.

"Don't. I don't want it. I don't want, need, or desire a fucking thing from you or anyone else. I've had my quota for this lifetime." Then I pushed it toward him. He just stood there looking at me. I bent down and sat it on the porch. "Just leave me alone. I am nothing, and I would like to continue to be nothing."

I turned and walked back to my car. As I was pulling away, I tried to force myself not to look in the rearview mirror, but I did. He was still standing in the doorway, and a woman had walked up and had her hand on his arm. But he didn't look at her. His eyes were on my car. I turned out of the drive and that was it. He was gone.

When I came back here, I made a huge pot of chicken noodle soup, and here I sit writing all this shit down, just to meet a fucking word count that I don't want to make. But for some strange fucked up reason, I'm doing it.

As with any place with no clock, no television, and no radio, time seems to mean nothing. It means nothing to me. It's light out so it's day, but it gets dark out pretty quick here, so it feels like night most of the time. So, sleep is what I have been doing. I am still so fucking lost, so full of anger. I've turned into a spiteful bitch. That brings a small smile to my face. I'm not this person. I'm not this person. John would be so disappointed in the woman I have become. What hell does he expect? He's gone. I can't even feel him anymore. I can't remember his voice, his words. It's all gone. My children are not even present in my mind, but I feel the loss of them in my heart. They are so faint, their lives so short. There just wasn't enough time to make enough memoires to sustain this gap in time.

I want to be dead. I wish for it every fucking day.

◦∽◦

Okay, you aren't going to believe this shit. So, I had a mental breakdown. Screaming, crying, I nearly threw this fucking albatross across the room.

Well, apparently, it snowed again, a great deal from the looks of it. While I was screaming, Ella's human was out there doing his good deed of shoveling. I guess my screams scared the shit out of him, because he kicked in my door to find me laying on the floor destroyed.

He managed to pick me up and wrap his arms around me. He didn't say anything, just held me. I didn't have the energy to push him away or to fight him, so I just laid there, limp in his arms, where he had me pulled against his chest, and let it all go. Well, I let go of all that I had at that moment. I think I fell asleep, because I woke up in my bed, which I hadn't slept in. When I got up and came out of the bathroom, he was sitting in the only chair I had.

There was a fire in the fireplace. I didn't even know I had wood. But there it was and sleeping on the rug in front of it was Ella. I stopped just shy of the living room. His head came up, and he smiled a small smile.

"I know you don't want me here, but you scared the shit out of me. I only stayed to make sure you were all right." He was very sweet.

Don't ask me why, but my eyes filled with tears. "I will never be all right. I will never be anything but nothing. Thank you, but please just leave me alone."

"Listen, I don't want to invade your privacy, but Ella comes here every day. I don't know why, but it means something to her." I turned and looked at her. She had her head on her legs, and she was looking at me. "None of this is my business, but I'm here, even if it's to just to have someone around."

I turned my head to look at him. "Why are you doing this? What do you want from me? I have nothing. I am nothing."

He chuckled. "I don't want anything."

"You should go. Thank you for shoveling, but you don't need to do this. I survived last winter, and I will survive next winter. I shop for the whole winter, so I don't have to go anywhere, so please stop."

He just sat there looking at me. When he stood up, I realized how tall he is. He walked up to me, but I took a step back. "Tell me your name," he said so softly.

"I'm no one. I am nothing. Please, don't come back here again."

"I don't think I can do that."

He turned and put his boots back on, then picked up his coat, and I watched as he put it on. "I fixed your door," he said as he opened it. Ella got up, walked over to me, and leaned on my legs. Then she walked out the door, and he followed her. Turning, he looked at me for a very long time, then he just left.

I didn't realize I was holding my breath until I let it out. Two fucking winters. Two.

I sat on the couch. Actually, I laid on the couch and watched the fire he had built in my fireplace. To be honest, I wasn't sure it worked. Besides, it's too cozy, and I don't want warmth. I don't want cozy. I want to suffer in silence. I don't know how long I laid there. It was dark out when I heard her barking. I ignored her at first because I just wasn't in the mood. But she jumped at my door more than once. So, I dragged myself off the couch, with every intention on yelling at her to go away.

When I ripped the door open, there was blood on my porch. "What happened?" I asked, like she would answer me. She hasn't said a word in all the time we've known one another. She barked and ran off the deck, waiting at the bottom. Like an idiot, I just stood there looking at her. She ran up to the door again and barked at me, then ran down the stairs.

I think it was the fact that there was blood on my deck that shook me. She came back up and grabbed my pant leg, pulling me out the door, which snapped me back to reality. "Do you want me to go with you?" Stupid question, I know, but hey, I've never had a dog try to communicate with me before.

I put on my boots, grabbed my coat, hat, gloves, and keys, and followed her out. She ran out to the car and down the driveway. I got in my car and followed her down the road. It was covered in snow. I know the plows don't get out here until they finish all the other roads. She was running at top speed down the road.

She slowed down, and that's when I saw his car. He had hit a tree and lying close to his car was a deer. There was blood everywhere.

"Shit," I said as I stopped and put the car in park.

Jumping out, I made my way over to his car. His head was lying on the steering wheel, and the door was open. "Hey." I shook him, but nothing. How the hell was I going to do this? He was huge. I pushed him back and could see the gash on his head. There was blood everywhere. I leaned across him and unhooked his seatbelt.

"Rick." I had to use his name. It felt weird to say it. He was unresponsive. "Rick, come on. Wake up." He moaned. Thank God, because I know I wouldn't be able to drag him to my car. "Hey, come on. Let me help you."

I managed to get him to help me get him out of the car and into mine. I took him to his house since it was closer than mine, and we managed to get him to the couch, where he laid down and passed out. I cleaned him up and bandaged his head.

There was no denying that he had definitely burned the furniture. I built a fire in his fireplace like he did at my house, and I sat in the chair and waited for him to wake. As I watched him, I will admit that I noticed he is very good looking. I found myself more than once scanning his body, which pissed me off. I found some tea in his kitchen and made a few cups while I waited. Always, I watched him.

The hours passed, and I could feel myself wondering things about him. Why was he out here? What did he want from me? Why did he burn everything? What would I say to him when he woke up? Should I call an ambulance? Was there even an ambulance around here?

As the sun came up, I realized that I had sat there all night, looking at him. I couldn't help but wonder if he had looked at me like this while I slept. Doesn't matter. I might be nothing, but at least he didn't freeze to death.

I needed to use the bathroom. When I walked back out, he was sitting up with his hand on his head. I just stood there like a statue. Ella was leaning on him. "Hey, girl. How'd we get here?" he said to her.

She barked and turned to look at me. When he lifted his head and smiled at me, my breath caught in my chest. "Thank you."

I nodded. "I had some of your tea." It was the only thing I could think of to say. "Your car is still on the side of the road. I can see that you are going to be fine." I moved toward the door, where I put on my coat and boots. I needed to get out of there.

"Wait," he said. "You don't have to go." I kept moving. As I opened the door, I felt him walk up behind me. "Please, tell me your name," he said softly.

With my hand on the door handle, I closed my eyes. "Becca," I said as I walked out. I moved as fast as I could, got in my car, and came home.

Now, here I sit, pissed off. I don't want to know him. I need to sleep.

CHAPTER SIX

So, I'm not sure how long I slept, but knocking on my door woke me up. I exhaled, knowing it was him. I didn't want to answer it, but the knocking wouldn't stop. I got up and ripped my door open, ready to tell him off for bothering me, but it wasn't him. It was that woman I saw at his house when I returned the gift he gave me.

I stood there looking at her. "Can I help you?"

"Hi, my name is Alice. Richard is my brother," she said, like I was supposed to know her or something. I just stood there looking at her. "I wanted to come and say thank you for helping him. He's doing better. I don't know what we would have done if anything happened to him."

I shook my head. "You're welcome." I went to close the door.

"Wait." She sounded panicked. "Do we know one another?"

I chuckled. "I doubt that very much. Now, if you'll excuse me, I need to get back to sleep."

"Of course, I'm sorry to disturb you. I just wanted you to know how thankful we are and to invite you to dinner tonight."

I stood there looking at her. "I'm busy, thank you." I closed the door in her face and went back to the couch. The minute I pulled the blanket over my head, she knocked again. "Go away!" I yelled. But she didn't.

I opened the door, ready to scream at her to leave me the fuck alone, when she said, "You're Becca Storm."

I swear, all the wind left my lungs. I felt like I was going to pass out. How the fuck did she know who I was? "Please, just leave me alone." I shut the door and burst into tears.

It's been two fucking years. How could she possibly know who I am? This is too much. I didn't want anything to do with him to begin with, and now, his fucking sister knows who I am. What the fuck! I'm going to have to leave here. I want nothing to do with this.

Not sure how much time has passed, but he showed up. I wanted to be rude and mean, but he just looked so damn sweet. Yes, I let him in, but only because… Well, I don't have a reason. It was what he said to me that blind fury came raging out of my mouth.

"Can I please come in?" he asked.

Ella stood beside him and waited. She wasn't her usual pushy self. I moved so he could come in. He didn't move past the door. Me, well, I walked into the middle of the room. He didn't take off his coat or his boots and Ella sat on the rug next to him. We didn't say anything for a long time. We just stood there staring at each other.

"I don't know how to begin," he said, stumbling with his words. "I wanted to thank you again for helping me, and I'm sorry for my sister. She told me she came over here to thank you."

I swallowed. He knows.

His eyes dropped to the floor. *Please, don't say it. Please, don't say it.* I kept thinking. When he picked his head up, I could see his eyes watering. "She told me who you were and what happened to you."

God, I was pissed. "Nothing happened to me," I snapped.

In a voice I barely heard, he said, "To your family."

"You need to leave. Go. You're welcome for my help, but please leave."

"Becca," he started.

"No!" I screamed.

"She said you disappeared over two years ago. Have you been out here alone for that long?"

"There is nothing about me you know. Just, please go." I could feel the tears coming.

"I understand now why Ella comes here. You need her."

"I don't need a fucking thing," I snapped at him.

"Becca, no one can survive without..." he stopped.

"Without what? Without other people? Without human interaction? Without what?"

"Yes, to all of that. I want you to know that I am here, if..."

I busted out laughing, but it wasn't real laughter; it was more sarcastic fake laughter. "What? Do you think I am going to fall into your arms? That I am going to need you? Stop this. I have nothing. I want nothing. I am nothing. Don't you get that? Hasn't the fact that I am here told you that? It's over. It's all over."

I think I might have been a bit over dramatic, but he was pissing me off.

I watched him take a deep breath, as if he was bracing himself, steadying himself. "Becca..."

"Stop saying my name like you know me. You don't know a fucking thing about me. Please, just leave."

Shaking his head, he said, "I know who you are. I know what happened to you. I know about your family. I know that you can't survive out here alone."

I stepped forward, now even more pissed. "What makes you think I want to survive? What makes you think I give a shit what you think? I don't, on both accounts. I don't want to be here. I don't want anything except to be left alone." I could feel the tears coming.

He didn't move, and he didn't say a word. He just stood there with Ella next to him. "Let me be your friend," he whispered.

I shook my head. "I don't want you as my friend. I don't want anything."

"I'm not going to leave here until you agree to be my friend. You need someone. Two years, Becca. Two years. There is life after a loss such as yours. I know."

"You don't know a fucking thing. I don't want a life. I don't want anything."

"My wife was killed in a car crash. She was giving my best friend a blow job on a side street, and a truck hit them. She bit his dick off. They had been sleeping together for over a year, and I was too fucking busy to notice. I know how you feel. I know more than you think I do."

I wanted to laugh, but that would explain why he burned everything. I almost felt bad for him. But he didn't know shit.

"I'm sorry for you, but you don't know anything."

"I know guilt. I know pain. I know anger. Listen, I just wanted to say thank you and to extend the arm of friendship. I've been out here alone for, what, eight months now. I walked away from my life with serious trust issues. I'll go, but know that I am right down the beach if you want to come and hang out. We don't have to talk. I wanted you to know that you don't need to feel so alone while you are here. I won't stop Ella from coming."

I nodded to him as he turned to open the door. Ella came over to me and leaned on my legs. She licked my hand and then they left.

God, I am so pissed that someone found me, that someone recognized me. I just want to be alone. I deserve nothing in this life. Nothing.

It's been a very long time since I sat down here. I'm still in shock that neither of you have made an effort to contact me. Trust me, I'm grateful that you haven't. I suppose, Janet, that when I told you to leave me the fuck alone that you understood me. Why can't anyone else?

So, I went to sit outside today, and I realized that the snow is melting, and the lake is starting thaw out. I'm inclined to believe that months have passed. I haven't seen him or Ella. I'm glad. I just want to sit here and wait, for either the lake monster, who I'm not so sure exists, or death itself to come and take me.

I need to head into town. I'm afraid that I have depleted my supplies.

Well, this is interesting. Apparently, Janet, you have sent me a package. Not sure I am comfortable with this. Not sure I am going to open it. Yeah, I don't think I am going to. I put it in the corner, and that is where it is going to stay. I hate surprises.

I got everything I need for another month, and well, I think I might just go back to sleep. I'm hoping to not wake up. But as with each time I close my eyes and hope... Huh, I have hope. Well, there you go. Each time I close my eyes with hope, I open them to disappointment. Story of my life.

The weeks have passed, and the snow is gone. Trees are growing new blooms. Spring is here, so back to the porch I went today. My Border Collie friend came to sit with me, and I was glad to see her. She stayed for a very long time. Even when I came in to get another cup of tea, she stayed, and then her human came to sit on the steps.

He didn't say anything. He just sat there looking at the lake. If I'm being honest here, and isn't that what this is, the truth of my life? I'm actually not disgusted with the way he looks. He really is quite attractive.

Paula, I think he would be your type.

I couldn't stop my eyes from looking at him. A few times, he would smile. I'm sure he could sense my staring. When I was finished, I reached down and gave Ella a pat on her head and then came in the house. I suppose they left. I didn't really check.

Another day, and they came to sit on my deck. This makes it more than a few times. I would say a week, but I don't count the days anymore.

"Why are you doing this?" I asked him while I looked at the water.

"I'm not sure. Maybe because I can't stand knowing you've been here for so long alone. Maybe because it feels good to just be with someone. Maybe because Ella seems to think you need some company. Like I said, I'm not sure."

"What do you hope to achieve by coming here?"

He chuckled. "I suppose that is a loaded question. I'm like you, just existing. So, why not exist at a certain time of the day together?"

I didn't know what to say after that. Did I like that he was here? I'm not so sure. Would I miss him if he wasn't? I might. I don't know what to make of him and his silence. He doesn't look at me like I look at him. He suffered a similar loss, but not really. But, then again, I don't know how he felt or feels about his wife, because I'm too shallow and bitchy to ask. I suppose, I shall consider asking him.

Today, I wanted to ask him about his wife, but then I realized that if I do, I am engaging him in conversation, which means he could ask me questions that I am not prepared to answer. I don't think I will ever be prepared. I can't, nor do I want to talk about them. The pain is just too fresh, too close to the surface. I don't want him to come here anymore. I don't want the company. I think I need to leave here.

It's been a while since I've been here. I got up the next morning and packed a bag and left. I went further north, looking for a new place, a place with no houses on the lakes. I found one, but it was kind of creepy. As I look around this one, well, Paula, you've never seen it, but it's not bad. Three bedrooms, which aren't slept in, two bathrooms, nice closets, but there aren't any clothes to put in them. The kitchen is nice, and the living room I would imagine is big. I only have a couch and a chair in it. My clothes are folded on the floor. Going in the bedroom is still too painful.

But this other house was like a dirt shack. I mean, yeah, it would be perfect for my glum demeanor, and it would probably be the perfect place for some crazy person to end it for me. But I would rather not be tortured and raped beforehand.

I've decided to go in another direction and see what lies there. I guess, when I return, I will let you know what I've found. Someone is knocking on my door. Bet you can't guess who it is.

Well, I opened the door to a pretty upset man and his trusty dog. "Where have you been?" he nearly shouted in his accusatory tone.

I stood there looking at him, not saying a word.

"I asked you a question."

Still, I didn't say a word. I wasn't sure if he was getting angrier or calming down. Not that it mattered to me which way it was going.

"You've been gone for more than a week."

I decided to put him out of his misery. "I'm not explaining myself to you."

"For over two years you have been here, and all of a sudden you get a gypsy bug in you and you take off."

I had to stifle a laugh. *Who the hell says gypsy bug?* I stood there waiting for him to figure it out. But, yeah, he didn't get it.

"I have asked you repeatedly to leave me alone. I want to be alone. I am nothing; therefore, I have nothing. I have nothing inside of me, nothing but anger and pain. There is so much pain that I can't think of anything. I have nothing. You won't stop. You just keep coming back. You don't own me. You have zero claim over me. I'm not worth this effort you seem to be putting forth. I've got nothing for you. So, I am going to do what I intended to do the first time around."

"What?"

"Please, just leave me alone."

"No, no one should be alone like this. Hell, you don't come out of the house for weeks at a time."

"Don't. Don't act like you care. You know nothing about me. You only know what your sister told you, what you read in the papers. You don't know shit. You think you know the pain of a cheating wife who died in some lover's embrace? You don't know shit. I need for you to leave."

"I'm not leaving. If I do anything else in this life, I am going to help you. You need someone."

I lost it. "I don't need shit! I don't want your help! Fuck you!"

I grabbed my purse and went to walk out of the door, and the fucking bastard grabbed me around the waist. "No," he said into my hair. "No."

I fought with him, but he wouldn't let me go. "Just, please," I tried to tell him, but then I started to cry. "Just, please, don't touch me."

"I'm not letting you go. You need to talk about this, to share the pain."

"I can't. I don't want to. I want it to consume me, to eat me alive."

His hold on me lessened. "Why?"

My head was so fucked up. "Because I left them," I whispered. "I left them."

And that was pretty much all I had left in me. I broke.

Sorry, I needed to breathe.

You're probably wondering what happened with my friend's human. I know he has a name, but using his name only makes him something to me, and he's not. I don't want to talk about what happened. Basically, I cried, he held me, then he put me to sleep and left.

I don't know why people don't understand why my solitude is what I want. It's what I need. You guys understand. You guys don't ever come around.

Oh, Paula, you'll be glad to know I just passed fifteen-thousand words. Only sixty more to go, and just think, it only took the better part of a year to get here. At this rate, you should have your book, in what, three and half more years. Lucky girl.

I've decided that both of you suck. I'm glad these words will be the last contact we have. If you were me, I would have come, whether you wanted me to or not. But I suppose it's fine. I've proven to myself that I don't need anyone.

I'm entering my second summer, and I'm doing fine, still existing. I haven't seen my Border Collie's human since that day, and I am definitely fine with that. She still comes and sits with me. I guess she feels the need.

Now that it has warmed up some, I'm back to lying on the beach and waiting for the lake monster to come. I am almost convinced there isn't one. I thought about swimming out until I couldn't swim anymore, to just let it happen. Then again, I know John would be pissed that I didn't at least give life a try without him.

I've been trying for two fucking winters. I can't do this. I can't survive this pain. It's never ending. It's all consuming. Maybe her human was right; maybe I just need... NO! I don't need. I can't need. I don't want anyone that can be taken away. Not now, not ever. I've lost my love, my heart. It's broken, and time isn't healing this wound.

I need sleep. I need to become Rip Van Winkle. Why can't I be like him? Why can't I sleep for a hundred years and not care? I'll tell you why, because life sucks.

I don't know how many days have passed or what the hell is wrong with me. I think I'm depressed. I suppose that is to be expected. Everything I love is now gone. It's been gone for so long that it doesn't even feel real now. I've been bogged down with internal agony that I haven't a clue which way is up anymore. I sleep most of the time, wanting or trying to bring them to my dreams, but nothing comes, just this total blackness, this total emptiness of absolute nothingness.

For the first time in so long, I looked at myself in the mirror this morning, or afternoon. I'm not sure what this moment in time is, but I don't even see myself anymore. I'm so thin that my face looks like a hollow shell. My hair is dull and in need of some serious hair products. My skin is white, almost translucent. I can see the veins.

I'm a mess, ladies, I think more so than I was after it all happened. I am literally dying here. I guess, in some sort of sick way, that pleases me, but in my heart, I know John is disappointed in me for giving up. I keep wondering if he would carry on in life if it was me. I'm sure he would have eventually. Is it eventually yet? Is it time for me to wake up?

When I went to walk to my spot on the beach, my feet kept moving. I made it to the edge of the hedge and just stood there looking at his house. I don't have any right to be there, any right to expect anything from him. The pile of ash and half burnt furniture still sits on the sand just past his yard.

When I finally looked away, he was standing on his patio looking at me. He nodded at me with a small smile. I nodded back. I couldn't bring myself to walk up there, and I couldn't find it in me to walk away. So, we just stood there looking at each other.

If I'm being honest here, and that's what this is about, he is quite attractive. His scruffy whiskers have been trimmed, and his hair is longer than it was the last time I saw him. He held up his cup to me, and I nodded.

I watched as he went back in the house and came out with another cup. He made the move to come to me. Handing me the cup, he smiled. Like a dork, I took it and sipped the tea. I shouldn't have been shocked to taste the same tea I drink. It kind of made me feel good that he made an effort to find the tea I like.

We didn't talk, just stood there looking at the lake, drinking our tea. Well, I don't know if he had tea in his cup. Somehow, he doesn't strike me as a tea man. He is much taller than I am. I think I might come up to his chest. He smelled good.

When I finished my tea, I handed him my cup. "Thank you," I said. "Anytime," he replied softly.

Then I turned and came home. I know he watched me walk all the way back to my house because I could feel him. I didn't see Ella today; I think she knew to just let it be. But I made an effort. I took a step that I'm not comfortable with, but I need to do what my husband would want me to do.

If it hadn't been for the reality of what I saw in that mirror, these words might have been a bit different.

Well, ladies, I did it again. I managed to find myself at the edge of the hedge. He was waiting for me this time. He nodded as he did yesterday and walked into the house, returning a couple minutes later with a cup of tea. This time, I sat down facing the water.

We didn't talk for a long time. "Thank you," I said softly.

He smiled. "Anytime. Did you want another cup?"

I shook my head and set my cup on the sand. I wrapped my arms around my legs, resting my chin on my knees. "I'm sorry I have been so mean to you."

"I'm sorry about the fire, for scaring the shit out of you. And you aren't mean."

"I am, and yes, you did scare the shit out of me. But it wasn't because of you; it was because of the..." I couldn't say the word. I didn't want to say the word.

"I have a truck coming later today to haul everything out of here."

"Well, that will be nice for you. Then you'll have your unobstructed view of the lake back."

He laughed. "I suppose I will."

I let go of my legs and stood up. "Thank you for the tea."

He looked up at me and nodded. Me, well, I turned and walked back to this house. Back to this stupid machine to continue to write on these pages to meet your damn quota.

I've thought about making contact with you both, but I don't think

I'm ready. I know you, Janet. You will want me to come back to civilization, and I'm just going to have to relieve you of your job. I'm never coming back or going back. I am staying here. I've learned how to survive through the winters, and no one bothers me here. Well, except for him and my friend the Border Collie.

My thinking seems to be moving forward a bit. In my mind set, I mean. I can't disappoint John. He was my world. They all were. He would want me to live. I'm not living the way I have been getting on lately. It's been a long time now, and I still have my anger, which shows up at the most inopportune moments. And my grief. I think they will linger just inside me for the rest of my life. My heart is still a stone in my chest. I'm pretty sure it will never flutter again, not the way it did for John or my children.

Why does life throw us such curve balls? Why do horrible things happen to good people? John was a wonderful man; a kind, caring, loving man, and he's gone. My children, innocent to the world, knew only love. But they are gone. I just don't understand any of this. I need to sleep.

CHAPTER SEVEN

So, a few days have passed, and I haven't been back to the end of the beach. I'm not sure how I feel about being near him. He doesn't make me feel uncomfortable, but I feel as if I'm doing something wrong. John would want me to move forward with my life, but I'm not so sure moving forward with another man is what is best for me.

I'm not over this gut-wrenching pain. So, I need to just stay by myself. I'm sure he is a perfectly wonderful man, but he isn't John.

Paula, why don't you come for a visit? Why don't you come and take him away, so I can wallow in my own self-pity like I have been?

I know I said that I should do more to be alive, but it all keeps pulling me back. Pulling me into the darkness and trust me when I tell you this. I love it there. If I could change one thing, it would be that they are there with me. But they never come. They never come to my dreams.

Now, I've limited myself to just sitting on my porch but not at my usual times. I've discovered that I might have thoughts concerning my Border Collie friend's human. He is very careful with me, with the way he talks to me. I'm not sure how I feel about that. I'm not sure I should be thinking about him or having thoughts about him. I mean, come on, we are the only two people within a twenty-mile radius.

What does he want with me? He told me that he was going to make sure I wasn't alone anymore, that he was going to help me. Help me? What exactly does that mean? Do I need help? Probably. Do I want help? No, I really don't. I would become dependent on him for my own salvation. I need to do this on my own. I need to find the thread of life that I'm supposed to grab onto to save myself. But I'm not so sure I want to be saved.

Don't get me wrong, I know that if I keep on living the way I am, that in another full four seasons, I might not survive. I mean, hell, you can see through my skin. I close my eyes and ask John repeatedly what I should do. Should I go back over there and start to have conversations with him? Should I try to be friends with him? Would it turn into something more? He is very good looking, and his eyes are drool worthy, if I was looking for that sort of thing. But I feel nothing. No warmth, no excitement. With John, it was... I don't know... Different.

When you move on in life, after such a setback, do you look for the same thing you lost? Is it ever the same? I would imagine it isn't. Is losing your life like breaking up? I can remember breaking up with guys. It hurt, sure, but it wasn't like this. Nothing is like this.

John, I could really use some advice here. I know you want me to have a happy life, but you and our children were my happily ever after. Weren't you? Or were you all just a part of my life that I was given for a little while. Is there something more? Am I supposed to do something more? Am I supposed to save him? Is he supposed to save me? I don't think I can do this. I don't think I have it in me to let you go. I love you. I will always love you.

Someone is at the door. Bet you can't guess who it is.

Here we go. I don't know if I'm floored or pissed. I'm going with pissed.

So, I opened the door, and yep, you guessed it. There he was. Rick.

"What happened? You stopped coming over."

I guess I gave him some kind of look, but I said nothing. I had nothing to say. So, I just stood there looking at him with my weird look.

"Did I offend you by assuming you wanted company?"

I nearly laughed but didn't because I'm pretty sure I would have burst into tears if I had. I didn't want to stare at him, but I would be lying if I said he wasn't something to stare at.

"Becca..."

"No!" I said rather loudly. "Don't. Just don't."

"Don't what?"

I shook my head, not really sure why him saying my name makes me so uncomfortable. I think it's the way he says it. It's a bit too sexy. He sort of whispers it. I don't like how it makes me feel. I know you're probably laughing right now, thinking, how could anyone not want a man to talk to her in a sexy voice? Well, I don't.

"Why are you here?" I asked him.

"I'm here because..." He smiled. "I'm here because..."

I raised my eyebrows at him. He was stuttering, trying to find his words. I'm sure he had something gushy to say but thought twice about it.

"I would like... Awe, hell, I could find a dozen things to say right now, but none of them would be appropriate."

I stood there thinking, *did I hear him right?* He was going to imply something more.

"I just... I just miss..."

By then, I knew I should put him out of his misery, but I didn't. I don't want to need him, and I certainly don't want him to need me. So, I stood there not saying anything, just watching him get even more uncomfortable.

"Will you say something, please?"

"I don't have anything to say." But I did. I had a great deal to say.

He took a deep breath, "I like having someone around, even if we don't talk. It's nice to just have another person around. I honestly don't know how you've been out here for so long alone."

I tilted my head. Really? He's lonely? I felt a bit uncomfortable with the underlying circumstances here. I was the only other person around. What exactly could he want from me? Then it hit me, and I got pissed. I think he saw my face change as I realized just what he was implying because he took a step back.

"I'm alone because I choose to be alone. I'm not your next step in life. I'm nothing. Don't you understand that? I've got nothing to give you."

"What? No, that's not what I meant. Shit, I knew this wasn't going to come out the right way. Please, Becca, that's not what I meant."

"Well, what exactly did you mean? We are the only two people out here, but if you want company, I'm pretty sure you wouldn't have a problem finding someone to keep you warm at night. I'm not her. I'm not it. I think it would be a good idea if you left right now."

"No, I don't want to leave, and I don't want someone in my bed. Hell, I don't even have a bed. It was the first thing I tossed on that pile. I'm just like you. I sleep on the couch. I want to hang out with you. I want to get to know you. Jesus, I can't stop fucking thinking about you over here all alone."

I yelled, "I like being alone!"

"At one time, I would have believed you. I don't believe that anymore. You came over. You feel the same as I do."

I laughed my sarcastic laugh. "You have no idea how I feel. I came over because I've been such a bitch to you, and it's not your fault. It's mine. I just want to be left alone."

He stepped forward. "No," he whispered. Another step. "I don't believe that." He stepped forward again, causing me to step back and let go of the door. He stepped again and kept moving until I was against the wall and he was inches from me. "You can't stay out here alone anymore. I'm not going to let you destroy yourself." His hand came up, and he put my hair behind my ear. I mean, it wasn't horrible to feel him touch me. "I've read your books," he whispered. "You are so talented. You can't just let yourself wither away to nothing."

I picked my head up, the tears falling. "It's because of those fucking books that my life ended. Everything you read was because of them. Because of him. He gave me that life. He gave me that love. He invoked that talent, not me. I left them, and then they left me. Never again. Never again will I care about something, someone. I wasn't meant for anything."

"No, that's not entirely true, and you are learning that. I know what it feels like to love someone like that, and then they are gone. My rage, my anger may not be as deep as yours, but my guilt is. I loved my wife, but she didn't love me enough. He loved you enough. I'm so sorry that this has happened to you. But I'm here, in whatever capacity you need or want. Our lives aren't over. This isn't the end."

I should have pushed him away. I wanted to push him away, but I couldn't.

"How? I've been trying for years to get beyond the anger, the guilt. It's still the same as it was."

His hand touched my face, his thumb wiping my tears. "Let me help you," he whispered.

I nodded, licking my lips. His beautiful bluish-green eyes closed slowly, and his head bent down. I could feel his breath on my lips. I swear, my heart stopped in my chest, and I prayed he wouldn't kiss me. Then he was moving away.

"I just needed you to know. I'm right down the beach, whenever you're ready."

I nodded, and he walked out the door, closing it softly. My whole body shook as I stood there. I am grateful for that wall.

You'll be glad to know that I didn't go down there the next day or the day after that. It's been a few days actually. I'm not sure what to do, how to think. Now, when I close my eyes searching for that darkness I love being in, his eyes are there, the warmth of his breath.

I can't do this, can I? No, I can't let him in. I can't let him get close to me. Is what he said true? Am I done being alone? In all honesty, I did enjoy sitting with him and drinking tea. I mean, it wasn't horrible. He was very careful when he put my hair behind my ear. He seems genuine. I think he might feel genuine. But how do you know? There should be some kind of test or something. Some magical way to tell if a guy is genuine.

I'm going to have to go down there. He made the effort to come here and see me, talk to me. He bared his emotions to me. I saw the sorrow and the pain in his eyes. I knew John was a good guy, but can I tell if he is? Well, ladies, we are going to find out.

I managed to make the walk down the beach to the hedge. I stood there for a few minutes but nearly turned around. I couldn't bring myself to walk up to his house. He did make an effort to come to mine, but I'm not needy for company. It's not who I am, so I took a few steps further away from the hedge. He did have the pile of uncharred furniture taken away. So, I decided I wasn't going to make him right, and sat down facing the water instead.

After a little bit, my Border Collie friend came up and leaned on my shoulder. I leaned back, and she sat down, putting her head on her legs. I was leaning back on my hands, looking across the very calm lake, wondering where the lake monster was and why it hadn't come to make a meal of me yet. When I looked down at myself, I realized how thin I've become. Thinner than I have ever been. I can see my hip bones, and my panties are too big for me, my bra as well. But, hey, I'm not going to complain about losing some of these boobs. At my normal size, I was a D cup. Now, I'm probably like a C.

We sat for a while before her human came. I know you are thinking the man has a name, but I still find it hard to use it. I think, in my mind, if I use his name, then we have some sort of connection, and I don't want that.

Who the hell am I kidding? I was there in front of his house, sitting in the sand with his dog, and he came strolling up. We have a connection. I'm in denial, I suppose.

So, he sat a few feet away and handed me a cup of tea. I looked at it, then at him. Taking the cup, I had to ask, "How do you know what kind of tea I like and how I drink it?"

"Well, I saw the tea on your counter, and I didn't notice any sugar."

"What if I liked milk?"

He smiled. "There was a cup that was half-full on the counter, and it didn't have any milk in it."

I didn't say anything. He is very observant, too observant if you ask me.

"What else did you notice while I was sleeping?"

He chuckled. "That your fridge has barely enough food in it, and your freezer has even less."

I sat there waiting for the lecture I'm sure he wanted to give me. But that was all he said about it.

"Also, after I put you in the bed, I realized that you sleep on the couch. I'm sorry I did that. Can I ask you why you don't sleep in the bed?"

He was getting personal, wanting me talk about them. I can't do that. I felt sick to my stomach, so I sat the cup down, stood, and headed back here. I can't and won't talk about them. By the time I got back here, he was sitting on my deck. This is ridiculous and becoming a bit annoying.

"Why won't you just leave me alone?" I asked him.

"Because I can't. I can't let you do this to yourself."

Shaking my head, I told him, "It's not your problem. I am nothing to you."

He stood up and stepped forward. "That's where you are wrong. All of this is wrong, Becca, and you know it."

"It's not wrong. It just is."

"Why don't you sleep in your bed?" he whispered.

I shook my head again. "I'm not going to discuss this with you. I don't ask you personal questions, so you shouldn't ask me."

"I don't sleep in my bed. Well, I don't have one anymore, but I didn't because it was the bed I shared with that lying bitch who cheated on me."

"Don't you have a life somewhere? Shouldn't you go back to it?" I wasn't so sure I wanted him to go. I wouldn't get to see my Border Collie friend if he left. Yeah, that's what I keep telling myself.

He gave me an odd look then. "No, no life. I sold everything I owned except for this house, and I walked away, just like you."

"I didn't walk away. I had nothing left. I still have nothing, and I still want nothing. If I don't have anything, then nothing can be taken away."

"Becca, you can't honestly think that way."

I walked past him, shaking my head. "It really is none of your fucking business." He pissed me off.

As I passed him, his arm wrapped around my waist and he stepped into me, pulling me against his body. I tried to get away, but he wouldn't let me go. "Tell me why you won't sleep in your bed."

I shook my head.

"Becca, please, let me help you. Tell me."

I felt the tears coming. "Because I wake up and he's not there. He will never be there again. He didn't walk away from me because he could; they were taken from me."

He removed his arm, and I came in the house and shut the door. Curling up on the couch, I cried myself to sleep. When I woke up, I sat down in front of this machine and wrote. I am nearing twenty thousand words, my quota getting closer.

Be careful what you wish for, Paula. You may not like what you get.

I don't know how many days I slept. When I wasn't sleeping I was plotting on how to feed him to the lake monster and keep his dog. I was angry at him for intruding in my misery. I didn't ask him to be here for me, and I don't want him here for me. His dog, that's our connection. So, perhaps, I should disassociate myself from the dog.

You know, this is bullshit. Why do I have to change my pathetic life because he thinks I should? I mean, I was fucking here first. I don't care if he owned his house before me. I was here first. Now, I'm going down there, and I am going to tell him exactly that.

Well, that went not at all like I planned. I got up and headed down to his house, but I suppose I'm some kind of nut job and have literally lost my mind. Nowhere in the book of this life does it say you can exist on only tea and sleep. I was nearly to the tall grass when I got dizzy. It was the weirdest thing. I have never passed out in my life. Everything around me turned hazy, and then the thumping in my ears was deafening. The world spun and looked distorted, and then my vision was fading. To be honest, that's all I remember, until I woke up to see him kneeling on the floor next to me with a cool rag on my forehead.

"What happened?"

"I'm not sure, but you scared the shit out of me."

Like I care how he feels.

"Ella was going crazy trying to get out the door. When I opened it, she took off barking her ass off. I followed her and found you lying in the sand. I brought you here and have been freaking out ever since."

"How long ago was that?"

"Couple of hours now. I was going to take you to the doctor's in town, but from the size of you, I figured you hadn't eaten proper in some time."

Well, isn't he special? God, I wanted to scream at him, but he was right. I pushed myself up, and he moved back. I didn't admit it to him, but I was still a bit dizzy. I gave him my hateful look. But he just smiled at me. Bastard.

"What I do really isn't any of your business. That's why I was coming here."

"To eat?"

"Not to eat, to tell you to back the fuck off. You have no right to touch me in anyway, especially forcing me to talk to you. I didn't engage this… whatever this is. You did. I want to be alone, which is why I bought that house out here away from everyone. I don't want to interact with you in any way, shape, or form, so please just leave me alone."

I pushed up to stand, but my head spun, and I wobbled. His hands came up to my hips, holding me steady. "Easy. Sit down and let me feed you. Please."

I pushed his hands off me. "Stop touching me."

I stepped away from him and headed to the door. but as I opened it, I stepped out on the deck and face planted. Stop laughing. It really wasn't funny. I slammed my head on his deck, and yes, knocked myself back out. Bitches, I swear, if you are laughing, I am so kicking your asses. Again, I woke up on his couch, this time with a headache. I could smell food cooking. He was nowhere to be seen, but the Border Collie was sitting vigil and barked when I pulled myself up to sit.

"Traitor," I whispered to her. She just smiled and wagged her tail.

I was working on standing but was getting nowhere. My vision was blurry, and I felt nauseated. What the hell? I felt like I had been drugged.

"Hey, hold on there. Just sit back down. I made you something to eat. You're not leaving here until you eat some real food. Then you can be all high and mighty and stomp off down the beach. But until you have food in you, you're not going anywhere."

I sat there giving him my evil bitch look. "You're not the boss of me!" I yelled.

He busted out laughing. I was shocked at how pleasing it was to hear. "No, I'm not, but I'm bigger than you and stronger than you, and damn it, Becca, you are going to eat. I'm not going to let you starve to death."

I was too weak to argue with him, and whatever he was cooking smelt wonderful. "Fine!" I snapped. I was really hungry. But he didn't need to know that.

When he went back into the kitchen, I closed my eyes, resting my head back on the couch.

Man, I think I fucked up. I think I am really starving myself. God, how do I get out of this? How am I supposed to just forget them and leave this pain that is literally killing me behind?

A few minutes later, he said, "Hey." I opened my eyes to see a plate with a steak on it with friend potatoes and green beans. "You need to eat."

I gave him my evil face again but took the plate. I can't tell you it was awful because I would be lying. It was so tender, so juicy, and so fucking good. I ate every damn bite. I cleaned my plate. It felt good to have food in my stomach, but I'm probably going to throw it up. It's been a long time since I ate like this. Years, I'm sure.

He got up and took my plate then walked into the kitchen. When I got up and walked to the door, I realized it was dark out. He came out of the kitchen. I looked at him. "Thank you," I said and opened the door. As I stepped out, I secretly cursed the fucking deck. Reaching up, I touched my head. Shit, I had a bump, and it hurt like hell.

"You don't need to go," he said from behind me.

I mean, he was right behind me. I felt him move, his arm wrapping around my waist again. What is it with this guy and my waist. He pulled me against his chest.

"Stay," he whispered.

I shook my head. Stay? He wanted me to stay. What the hell?

"Stay with me," he whispered again. I heard him take a deep breath, like he was smelling me. "I want you to stay. You can go home in the morning. It will give me another chance to feed you."

"Among other things," I said.

If I'm being honest, and isn't that what this is about? He was warm, and gentle, and smelled so fucking good. Better than the food. But, and there is always a but in situations like this, I am not an option for him and his rock-hard body that smelled just shy of heaven.

I stepped forward, and he let me go. But I didn't turn around. I couldn't; I didn't want to see the... oh, I don't know what word I would use here... Disappointment? Hurt? Sadness? It doesn't really matter, I suppose, because I want no part of this. Stay. What the hell, and exactly where would I sleep? On the couch with him? Yeah, no thank you.

As I reached the tall grass, my friend the Border Collie came running up. I smiled a little smile at the fact that he'd sent her to walk me home. When I started up the deck, I turned and looked at her. "Thank you," I said.

I swear, she nodded to me. Can dogs do that? Do they try to communicate? I know they bark when they want your attention, and they pull on your clothes, but do they really nod, or am I going crazy wanting to believe she can communicate? I suppose, in the big picture of things, it doesn't matter.

So, on my way home, I decided not to engage with him. Why does he touch me? I mean, I'm not naive, by any means. He is just horny, and I'm the only girl around. No fucking way is that going to happen. I need to sleep. I need for this to go away. I need to move.

My mind was sort of numb. All night long, or however long I slept or didn't sleep, he was there intermittently invading my darkness. His eyes, his scent, his touch... Why can't I feel my husband like this, or my children? I want them, not him.

The knocking on the door dragged me out of my slumber. I didn't want him to be here. How many times did I have to tell him I didn't want to do this? I literally rolled off the couch and crawled over to the door before opening it up.

"What do you want? Please, stop this. Please, just leave me alone."

He got down on his knees, setting a tray on the floor next to him. "I came to feed you again." He put my hair behind my ear.

"Why are you doing this?"

His fingers lingered on my face. "Because, whether or not you believe this, you need me to help you."

I sat back on my heels. "I don't need you. I don't want you to do this."

He smiled. I didn't notice before, probably because I've never been this close to him, and because he has this scruff on his face, but the man has fucking dimples. I mean, come on. He smells like fucking heaven, he is way too kind, has eyes a girl can get lost in, and he has fucking dimples. Really?

"Come on. Put some clothes on. I spent all morning making you breakfast."

I watched as he stood, taking the tray with him to the kitchen. Me, well, I wanted to throw one of my angry fits and slam the door, screaming at him, but whatever he had on that tray smelled delicious. Kind of like him.

God, why am I thinking like this? Am I horny, too? Probably, but I want John. I know. Stop my fucking whining and move on. John has been gone for two years now. He would have moved on already. I know, because I know his sexual appetite. It was every day, and some-times, he would even wake me up in the night. Not that I ever complained. The man was beyond anything I had ever experienced.

I got up and went to the bathroom, brushed my hair and teeth, and changed my clothes. Like I have a great deal to choose from. When I walked out, he had two plates ready, both filled with eggs, bacon, and homemade cinnamon rolls, complete with icing.

Like the bitch that I am, I stood there looking at the plate instead of taking it and being thankful. He set the plate on the counter. As he passed me, he leaned down and said in my ear, "I'm not leaving until you eat." I know he was smiling. Bastard.

Oh, you're fucking right I ate it, just so he would leave, but I didn't join him in the living room. I stood in the kitchen at the counter and ate. It was so fucking good, especially the cinnamon rolls. Hell, he looks like that, smells like heaven, and the bastard can fucking cook.

He was right. When I finished, he smiled, left the rolls, and took everything else home with him. On his way out the door, he stopped and said, "I'll be back for lunch. Did you want to eat on the beach or here?"

I gave him my evil face. "I don't want lunch," I snarled at him.

He walked up to me, put his hand on my chin, and tilted my head up. "Too bad. I'll see you in a few hours."

And just like that, he was gone. I know he walked out of here with that smug ass look on his face. What the fuck am I going to do? He is forcing himself into my life, and it would seem that I am letting him. I don't want to let him. Well, that's what I keep telling myself. But, and there is always a fucking but in situations such as this, I think I might enjoy him.

Okay, so I know you bitches are jumping up and down now, thinking I'm coming back from my black hole. But I'm not. When he left, I slept. You're wondering, I'm sure, if he came back for lunch. Of course, he did, just as he said he would. And, yes, he even came back with dinner. I will give it to him, the man is persistent. But it was what happened after dinner that will definitely make you squeal with delight. I could just tell you, but then what fun would that be? I am still so pissed about it all. I hate when people assume that the things they say or do are acceptable to those around them, just because they are cute.

So, we finished dinner. Keep in mind that I only ate it because he threatened to stay if I didn't, and yes, before you ask, I stood in the kitchen and ate. Well, when we finished, he packed up his things and sat them in the container he brought them over in that was by the door, and then he just stood there.

"Thank you for the food," I said to him. I was standing across the room. "It isn't necessary that you keep doing this. I am capable of feeding myself."

He smiled. "I know you are, but from what I can see, you don't. I told you I'm not going to let you do this to yourself."

Man, I was pissed. "It isn't your concern what I do. I didn't invite you into my life. Hell, I don't want you in my life."

To be honest, he is growing on me, but I wasn't about to let him know that. I think he does know it, though.

He smiled. "Becca, you're right. I invited myself into your life, into your world of darkness. I want to be here. I want to help you."

I gave him my evil face. "Why? Why should it matter to you what I do?"

"Because I am a human being, and I couldn't live with myself if I didn't try to help you. Someone has to. I know no one comes here. I know you go weeks without talking to anyone. I know you barely eat anything..."

I interrupted him. "How do you know these things? Are you spying on me?" I was being a total bitch.

He chuckled. "No, I'm not spying on you. You want the truth? I've seen pictures of you, and you are way too thin. You look like death warmed over." If steam could come out of someone's ears, it would have been coming out of mine. I was that pissed, but he wasn't done. "You are doing this because you are so sad, and I don't blame you one bit. I am amazed that you survived it all." His voice got softer, and he moved closer to me. I stepped back, but I was already against the wall. I think it took him three steps before he was in front of me. "But you did survive. You did." His hand came up to my face. It was so big that it covered the entire side of my head. "Don't cry." He wiped my tears I didn't know were there. "Don't cry. You're alive, and for whatever reasons, you are here."

"I don't want to be here," I whispered to him. I don't. I want to be with them.

"I know. I felt the same way. I was so embarrassed by what happened, but I was also in total shock at what happened. How was I so stupid not to see it? I was making love to my wife, and she was thinking of someone else. I know how you feel."

I shook my head. "No, you don't."

He tilted my head up and lowered his, whispering against my lips, "Yes, I do." Yep, you guessed it. He fucking kissed me. It wasn't a full on kiss, just a soft brush of his lips across mine. When he realized that my body went rigid, he pulled back a little. Not much because I could still feel the heat of his breath on my lips. "I do know. I'm going to go now. I'll see you for breakfast." He slowly let go of me and moved back to the door, where he picked up his container and then he left.

The bastard left me standing there, with tears running down my face, my body shaking. I haven't kissed anyone but my husband in thirteen years. What the fuck was that? On top of every fucking thing about him, his lips… Fuck, his lips are soft. God damn it, I am so mad.

Who the hell does he think he is? What gives him the right to kiss me like that? To assume I would be all right with it? Well, I'm not. I'll be back. I think it's time I kick ass and ask questions later.

So, I'm going to tell you what happened, but you better not laugh or think anything of it. I got in my car and drove over to his house. I don't think he was shocked when I knocked on his door.

"What the hell was that?" I yelled. "What makes you think you can just kiss me like that?"

He smiled. "This," he said, then reached out and wrapped his arm around me, pulling me up and into his body, before covering my mouth with is.

Okay, I'm not going to say it was horrible, because it wasn't. But I didn't kiss him back. I actually hit him a few times until he pulled away and sat me down. I slapped him across the face, and he smiled. He fucking smiled.

"What the fuck?" I screamed at him.

He just stood there, his arm still around me. Pulling me in, he shut the door and pushed me against it, leaning into me. I didn't feel threatened; it was just the opposite. To explain how I felt, well, I'm not sure I could.

"Becca, I'm not sorry."

I didn't know what to say. I think I was in shock, because the tears just came, and what did he do? What every fucking knight in shining armor does. He pulled me up his body and wrapped me in his warmth and held me while I cried. I don't know how we ended up on the couch, but he cocooned me in his body and held on to me.

It felt so good to feel his warmth and to just let it all go. I've cried for years now, alone in my darkness, but this, this felt different. He was doing all the right things, pulling me out of the dark. I fought it. I am still fighting it as I sit here. I want to feel the pain that reminds me of what I lost, what I don't have anymore. What I want.

He didn't say a word while we laid there. Not one word. I cried myself to sleep, still sobbing through the night, but he didn't let me go. To be honest, and that's what this is here on these pages, honesty. I didn't want him to. I think I needed to feel the comfort of a stranger. But he isn't really a stranger, is he?

I met a dog on the beach, and then I don't know how much longer, I was laying in the arms of her owner. When I opened my eyes, his trance-inducing bluish-green eyes were looking back at me. His hand was on my face, his thumb moving softly across my cheek. Not one word was said about what happened. I could feel his arm along the side of my breast, but I don't think he noticed when he leaned in and kissed me. I felt his tongue gently brush along my lips, and God help me, I gasped a little and my mouth opened unintentionally. I'm sure he thought it was my way of giving him my approval to continue. It wasn't. I swear to God, it wasn't. I was just shocked that he did it. He, so slowly, so sweetly, so gently kissed me proper. I let him. Hell, I engaged him, and it felt so good to share this with him.

His kiss was different from John's first kiss. His wasn't cautious; he knew what he was doing, and I felt it. John's was more of a 'should I do this'? Rick's was full of 'I want this, and I'm not stopping'.

When my hand moved on its own, during this kiss, to his face, and then into his hair, the kiss deepened. His leg moved between mine, his hand made its way to my thigh, and he pulled it over his and pushed into me, deepening the kiss. I was lost, lost in the feeling of light, of warmth. He was dragging me out of the darkness. I couldn't let him do that. I had no control over the tears as they fell from my eyes. I stopped engaging him. The betrayal I felt was so overpowering. I was cheating on my husband. I promised to love only him.

He pulled back, his hand still on my thigh. "I'm not sorry," he whispered. Hell, even his breath was wonderful to smell. Who the hell is this man?

I nodded and moved to untangle us. I managed to get up and just walked out the door and came home. I left my shoes there.

What the fuck? I can't do this. I don't want to do this. I need to leave. The scary house alone on the lake up north is looking very good right about now. I packed a bag. Don't know when I'll be back.

Don't worry, Paula. You'll get your seventy-five thousand words. I just passed twenty-three thousand, and for some reason, I don't think this is over.

So, yeah, you aren't going to believe this. Actually, you probably will. I opened the door to leave with my bag in hand, and who was standing there? Yep, you guessed it, the Border Collie's owner. He just stood there looking at my bag, his eyes slowly moving up my body, and let me just say this. I felt it.

"Where are you going?" he asked. He actually looked a bit hurt.

I didn't say a word, just gripped my bag handle a bit harder.

"Becca, don't do this. Don't run."

I tilted my head, giving him my evil face, because damn it I was pissed. Why does he think he can just assume that I'm going to drop my bag and throw myself into his arms? Trust me when I tell you, they are very adequate arms.

"It doesn't matter. I can't do this. I don't want to do this. I love him. I will always love him. Nothing else matters."

"As I will always love my wife, but they aren't here anymore. Do you think he would have moved forward if it happened to you? Do you think he would want this for you, to stay locked in this house, to starve yourself to death?"

He had a point. I know John wouldn't have wanted this for me.

"What happens to me is none of your business," I snapped.

Shaking his head, he smirked. "You stupid woman," he said as his hands came up and grabbed my head, pulling me toward him. His mouth covered mine, and he kissed me. I mean, really kissed me. He didn't wait for my mouth to open; he shocked the hell out of me, so my mouth was already open.

I don't know what the hell happened, but my bag hit the floor, and the next thing I knew, he was picking me up, my legs instinctively wrapping around his waist. He turned and leaned us against the wall. When he pulled back, both of us were breathing a bit heavier than we should have.

"I want it to be my business. Let me make it my business," he whispered on my lips, then kissed me again. My hands were in his hair.

Ladies, the man can kiss. But these kisses aren't mine. They aren't the ones I want. Don't take this the wrong way, because the man is magnificent, but he's not John. He's not my husband.

I pulled back, my head hitting the wall. "No, you're not him. You're not my husband. I love John. I love him."

He put his forehead on my chest. "And I love my wife, but they are gone, Becca. Both of them. How are we expected to live like this, without someone to share life with?"

The tears came. "I don't know. I've been trying to figure that out. I don't know. I didn't ask for this, to be alone without them. I want my family, my children, my husband."

Raising his head up, he tilted mine down. "I know, but I'm here. I'm right here. Let me share this with you. Tell me about them. Share them with me."

"I can't," I cried. "I can't even look at their pictures. Oh, God, I miss them so much I can't breathe."

"Let me help you. Let me share them with you."

He kissed me again, and I let him. His hands moved into my hair. Our mouths melded together. All of my pain I gave him in that kiss. It lasted a very long time, the dance or fight of our pain slowly subsiding, and the kiss took on a life of its own. We slowly stopped.

"Please, don't leave. Don't run." I nodded. He pulled us back from the wall and set me down. "I brought some food. Let me go get it. We can eat and talk. Okay?"

I nodded and watched him walk out the door. I went to the bathroom and washed my face. I suppose it's time to talk about them. To tell someone.

We had a lovely picnic on the living room floor. He told me about his wife, how they met, why he loved her so much. I told him about

John and how we met. It was hard at first to get the words out, but once they started coming, I couldn't stop them. Every once in a while, he would reach up and put my hair behind my ear. He listened attentively, never interrupting.

When I finished talking, he grabbed my hand and brought to his lips. "I can see why he loved you instantly. I almost envy him, that he found you first. But I am glad that he loved you the way you should have been loved."

Now, what kind of man says that? I mean, fucking swoon-worthy, right? What the hell?

"I'm sorry she didn't love you enough."

His hand came up and wrapped around my neck, pulling me toward him. "I'm not." He kissed me, pushing us backwards until I was on my back.

I could get very used to this. Is this how I move forward? Just do it? Just let him lead me, when I'm not sure I want to be led? I pulled away from him and rolled over, getting up. He laid on his back, looking up at me.

"I don't want to do this. I can't do this."

I felt like a broken record. I felt like I was betraying my husband.

"We aren't doing anything wrong."

"Yes, we are. I am cheating on him. I am wanting things with you that I only had with him. This is wrong. You need to go."

I watched as he got up. "Becca, I don't want to leave. I want to stay."

Shaking my head, I moved further away. I wanted him to leave. "I can't."

"You have been. He's gone, just like Julia. They are gone, and they are never coming back." His words were gentle and kind.

"I'm just the only one here. Go. Go back into the world and find someone who can give you what you want. I'm just the only one here."

"No, there is nothing left for me there. Like you, this is all I have left, just me, just the empty man before you. Let me help you, Becca. Let me in."

"Don't you understand? I can't. It's not right. I can't betray him like that."

I wasn't expecting him to react the way he did. He walked to the door and put his shoes on. Turning, he said, "I'm right here when you're ready."

"What if I'm never ready?"

He was across the room, picking me up again and carrying me to the couch. "You're ready," he whispered as he kissed me. And, yes, I kissed him back. He's a remarkable kisser. "You're just scared, and that's all right, because I'm fucking terrified." He laid me on the couch, turned, and walked out the door.

I swear, I almost yelled for him to come back. I didn't want him to leave. But he is right. I am terrified.

Yes, I cried. I always cry. it seems to be what I do best. Stay in my darkness and cry for the man I lost, the man I love, the children who were my heart. But he is right, and I fucking hate that. I'm sure you are all right, every last one of you. Enough time has passed, and shouldn't it be time for me to get moving? If it is, if everyone thinks so, then why can't I seem to do it? Why am I stuck here?

I slept for two days again. It wasn't John or my children in my dreams; it was him. His eyes, his lips, his breath. Why? I think I'm scared because he sees me. He sees right into my soul. He knows my pain; therefore, he knows me, only because I have become the pain. I am the pain.

I can still smell him, feel him, taste him on my lips. I can't do that with John anymore. I can't remember his voice or his touch. My memories are there, but they come with no real sound. Am I a horrible person for letting them go? Or is it time that is taking them away from me? Is he the one? Is he the reason I'm here?

When I first met John, I believed that about him, that we ended up staying at the winery because I was meant to be with him. But if he was my happily ever after, wouldn't he still be here? Wouldn't we still be living our life? Our beautiful, loving life.

Why is grief such a bitch? God, I have so many questions for the fucking universe, questions I'm sure every person who suffers loss asks. It's been days since I've seen him, not that I went looking. I should go over. I should just take a deep breath and go over there. But I'm terrified.

Janet, I know you would push me out the fucking door. You always seem to get me to do what I can't bring myself to do. But this is something I need to do for me.

Okay, so, I'm going now.

CHAPTER EIGHT

So, yeah. I don't even know what to say here.

Yep, I got nothing.

Okay, from the beginning. So, I put my shoes on, and I went over there. I tried to talk myself out of doing it. What I should have done was take my bag and get in my car. I mean, it's not like I can't afford to go anywhere in the world I want. Well, okay, I have no passport, but this is a big country. I know, I'm procrastinating.

I walked to the hedge and stood there for a few minutes. I'm really not sure why I was doing this. Well, that's a lie. I know why. John, he's why. What he said about John not wanting this life for me, well, it hit home. I should move forward. Saying it and doing it are two different things, that's for sure.

I made myself walk up to the door. I knocked, but he didn't answer. I walked around to the front, and his new car was in the driveway, so I went to the front door and rang the doorbell. I still don't understand why he has a doorbell when there is no one around. It was weird. I heard him yell out to hold on.

So, I stood there, waiting. When he opened the door, he was just wearing a pair of jeans, and he was wet. Yep, he'd been in the shower. I was taken back by his body.

Janet, you would have drooled.

Paula, I really don't care how much you love your husband; you would have taken a second look.

If I'm being honest here, not that I want to compare him to John, my husband didn't look this good.

He stood there for a second, looking at me. Then his arm came out of nowhere, scaring the shit out of me when he grabbed me around the waist and pulled me into the house, kissing me. His hands grabbed my legs as he picked me up. We were moving, but I couldn't tell you where the hell we were going. Honestly, I didn't care. He has the sweetest kisses.

When we finally stopped moving, his hands were on my face and in my hair. He pulled back and looked at me. "Hi," he said all breathy. Fuck if he wasn't the sexiest fucking man I've laid eyes on. Maybe it was that he didn't have a shirt on and he was wet. Yeah, that was it.

"Hi, I just wanted to come and tell you okay."

He laughed. "Yeah?"

I nodded. "Yeah."

I realized I was sitting on his thighs and we were on a bed. I looked around, and really, I felt completely uncomfortable.

"It was delivered yesterday. I figured it was time to sleep in a bed, but I haven't slept here yet."

I think the look on my face said it all for him. "Did you do this thinking I would share this bed with you?"

He shook his head. "No, I told you, I'm not looking for someone to share my bed."

"Then why did you bring me in here?"

I think he felt my body shaking, because he was very careful with his words. "Because it's the biggest piece of furniture I have, and I did hope that we could do this some more." He slowly kissed me, and I mean slowly.

He laid me back and then shifted his body so we were lying on our sides, looking at each other. "Please, don't think I would ever assume that this is acceptable, but when you are close to me like this, you seem to feel a bit more relaxed and you open up to me. It feels more intimate for me than sitting on the couch or the beach. I won't lie to you, but I think I would really love to make love to you. I also know neither of us is ready for that."

I shook my head. "No, not ready for that."

He smiled at me. "Good, there is so much more I want to know about you. So much more you need to know about me. I'm just glad you came over."

"This bed is very comfortable." What else was I going to say?

"I haven't laid on it until now, but it feels good. I have a confession to make. I did want you in here, on it with me. Now, when you leave, it will smell like you."

I felt my face heat up. I mean, come on. Either he is trying really hard to get me to take my clothes off, or he is beyond the sweetest man on the planet. I'm going with him trying to get me to take my clothes off.

We just laid there and talked, learning more about each other. I started to tell him about my children, but I'm not ready to share them with him. As much as I miss John, I miss them a million times more. They are a part of me, a part I'm not ready to share. Of course, he was very understanding. But, then again, I think he's in this to get laid. We shall see.

He made me dinner, and I did share some wine with him. Admittedly, I was a bit light headed, and I spent the night with him. Yes, as you throw your hands up to your mouth and gasp, we slept in his new bed. It wasn't planned. We were just lying there talking, with our clothes on, and I fell asleep. So, before you start screaming in happiness and joy, it didn't last long.

I knew it wasn't right for me to be in his bed. I mean, technically, he is a stranger. Yes, I know I slept with John after our first date, but I wasn't getting over a loss like this. I woke up and got out of bed. It just wasn't right. I left his house and started home. I was about halfway there when he ran up beside me.

"What happened?"

I hadn't realized I was crying. To be honest, I think I was crying because deep down inside it did feel right. I haven't shared a bed with a man who wasn't my husband in nearly fourteen years. This man was a perfect gentleman. I believed he didn't want anything but to get to know me. Maybe it just felt different for me. He feels different. Not wrong, but different. I am hanging on to my husband, trying to honor him and his memory. I feel as if I am betraying it, betraying him.

I shook my head. "Nothing."

"Becca, something happened to make you get up and leave like that."

I stood there looking at him, "I shouldn't be in your bed with you. I can't be that woman. I know what you want from me, and I can't give it to you."

"I don't want anything from you."

I felt like he was being a bit condescending towards me, talking to me like I was an idiot, and I got defensive.

I laughed my sarcastic evil laugh, "Do you really think I'm that stupid? You kiss me, more than a few times, with such passion, then you buy a bed and the first thing you do is take me to it, in a heated kiss. Of course you want something from me. I know because I want the same thing from you. But that doesn't mean it's going to happen. We are the only two people for twenty miles. Yes, I'm lonely, terribly lonely, but it's him I miss, it's them I want."

"What if I told you that I think I have feelings for you? Hell, I don't think, I know I do. I want more, yes, god, I want more. I want all of you. But not because you are the only woman around, and not because you make me so fucking horny I can't think straight. When you came over today, I had just finished jacking off in the shower, thinking about you. Not my wife, but you. That's why I reacted the way I did when I opened the door. I just wanted to kiss you, to feel your body against mine, to smell your sweet scent, to feel your warmth. Don't you get it Becca? I don't want someone else, I want you."

As I sit here remembering the look on his face, my eyes close. The sincerity in his words, in his eyes, was something I had never seen in a man, not even my husband. He was putting his heart on his sleeve.

"Rick…"

It came out in a shallow whisper, I wasn't even sure I said it. Not until I was in his arms and he was kissing me. I didn't fight him. He was moving, carrying me down the beach to his house. We ended up back in the bed.

It was the most surreal moment since this began. It felt as if I have known him my whole life. Something changed when I said his name. He knew it to. At that moment, nothing was between us, not his wife and not John. Our hands moved over one another's bodies like we had been doing it for years. He was so gentle, so caring. when his hand cupped my breast, I felt like I would burst into flames. My whole body warmed, and let me say, it hasn't felt warmth like this in years.

We weren't rush, we weren't desperate, we were kind, and tender, and very aware. He actually bit my lip when I brushed the back of my hand along his erection. And oh did I mention…OH MY GOD!! But again I have to say, that it was petting with our clothes on. We didn't hump one another, it wasn't like that.

When we finished, he pulled me into his chest and whispered, "Stay, don't leave. Just stay."

I did, I stayed for the whole night, the next day, and yes even the next night. We talked mostly, about nearly everything, he made me laugh a few times which I wasn't all that comfortable with, but it is what it is.

So now I sit here, thinking I might want to be there. I know in my heart that it's wrong to want something that I know can be taken away from me. I think I might have conditioned myself to believe I wasn't ever going to be worthy of having something like this again. He told me he wants me, but I can't stop thinking about the fact that I'm the only other person around.

If I let him in any further, he has the potential to destroy me, to end me.

It's been two days since I came home. Two days I've been pacing and sleeping, thinking about what I did. How I let him touch me, let him kiss me, let him hold me and the fact that I slept in a bed again, with another man who wasn't my husband.

If I close my eyes, I can feel him, hear his laugh, feel his breath on my lips, see the wonder in his beautiful bluish green eyes. It's not John anymore in my mind. What have I done? Is this normal to feel as if I betrayed his memory? I feel sick most of the time that I share intimate moments with another man. Somehow, somewhere, I think this is how people move on from tragedy. I suppose the question is, how do I feel about it? I can't answer that. I just know that right now in this moment I feel lonely.

Paula, don't you dare say "Awe," because this isn't an awe moment. I know Janet is squealing for whatever reason. No, I'm not coming back, I'm not writing any more than this. The stories are gone, they don't come anymore. It's been two years and I don't have it anymore. I'm just a one hit wonder ladies.

Another day has gone by, I went and sat on the beach for far longer than I would have, and my friend the Border Collie didn't come. I was going to go down to his house but I didn't want to seem needy. I don't want him to think that I can't live without him.

I just don't understand why he was so pushy to get to know me and then he just leaves me alone again. Come to think of it, I'm a bit pissed off. Yeah I'm going down there. Be back later.

Well that was a whole lot of energy wasted. He wasn't there, his car was gone. Maybe he went to town. I don't know, but I feel the need to be in the darkness. Funny I don't remember myself ever being this insecure before. I wonder what the hell happened to me. Why did I do this to myself? Am I so self-absorbed? I need to stop this cowering in the corner, and playing the poor me card. Life isn't like this. It's been two years, I can't do this anymore.

I think he woke something up inside of me, sparked my inner self. Maybe I should come back to reality, go back to the real world. Go back to California, back to the sunshine. I don't need to stay here and be my own victim. I'll give him a few days and then I think I should head back to reality. Yes, that's what I'm going to do. No one needs to know where I am. I mean Paula, I have the address to your office. I can just send this there when it's reached it seventy-five thousand words.

Yes, my Border Collie friend's human, Rick, pushed me and helped me. I suppose I should be thankful. I am very thankful to him for giving me the shoulder I needed, the leaning of his ear, to hear myself, to hear how pathetic I really am acting. I'm coming back to life ladies. Think it might be a little time for an adventure.

I've given him eight more days, and he still isn't there. So I've packed my little bag, I'm leaving everything here, no not the computer. It's coming with me. But my suitcase, and that mysterious box that sits in the corner, giving me it's evil eye when I look at it. No Janet I haven't opened it. Not yet, maybe after I take this first step back into reality. So, I'm heading off, ladies. We'll be in touch. Wish me luck.

I'm scared shitless and very hurt by what he did to me. But, you know, I have to believe that people come into our lives for a reason. Rick came into mine to get me to this place. At least, that's what I keep telling myself, even though I am going to leave here with a sad feeling inside of me. A feeling of total devastation, but I am leaving.

Sitting on this plane as we zoom back to the real world, I feel a bit nervous. I haven't used my real name in a very long time, so it was strange to hear someone say it. I booked a room at the Seasons until I can have the person I sublet my apartment to moved out. It will be a month, I'm sure. There is so much that I need to do to become whole again.

My mind wanders to Rick. Why did he leave me like that? Was he even real? Did I dream him up in my head? He was like an enigma in a sense. I really feel the loss of him. I suppose that's on me for believing he wanted this between us. It shouldn't matter. I kept telling him I couldn't do it, I didn't want it. But now, now, I'm sorry I left.

I've been here for three days, and I've eaten so much food. It's easy to do when you just pick up the phone and twenty minutes later it arrives at your door. I'm still plagued with thoughts of him, even though it's been nearly a month since I've seen him. I should have known better. I should have known he wasn't someone I could trust.

I've hired a car to take me out to the vineyard today. I thought it best that I don't drive. I'm pretty sure it's going to kill me, but I need to do it. I need to see where my life ended. Probably not the best thing to do, but I am determined to move along with this life, with what's left of this life.

CHAPTER NINE

It's taken me a week to be able to put these words here, to tell you what it felt like.

The closer we got to the vineyard, the greater the feeling of suffocation crept up. By the time we hit the long drive at the end of the property, I was nearly hyperventilating. I asked the driver to pull over, and I got out of the car.

I put my hands on my knees, with my back toward the land. Once I caught my breath, I looked out. The earth was coming alive. There was grass everywhere, but you could still see the scorch marks. Turning, I felt my breath catch. What once was a lush green valley as far as the eye could see was nothing but grass and weeds.

"I'm going to walk from here," I told the driver who got out of the car. He smiled at me.

My feet wouldn't move. I had to force them. I had to force myself to move forward. Step by step, I walked down a road I used to walk nearly every day with the kids to get the mail. I turned my head, looking, but even the mail box was gone. Everything was gone.

Step by step, closer and closer I got to where the house stood. I could see it in my mind. I could see the swing John hung in the tree for me. The swing my children played on. I eventually stopped in front of the area where our house once stood. Closing my eyes, I could hear them. I could hear their giggles, and John's bellowing laughter as he chased them around the house, around the yard.

The tears fell, but somehow, they didn't feel the way they did before. We had a good life, a happy life here. Their little voices are alive in me. I remember them. I remember how good it felt to hold them, to laugh with them, to play with them. It never left me. It was just drowned out by the darkness I felt. I feel full again. I feel alive.

The moments I hold dear to me played out in my mind. Them running out of the house into the yard, John following them laughing. I stood and watched in my mind. I followed them to the swing and then back to where our porch was, John standing there looking at me. In my mind, he smiled and nodded to me. It felt as if he was telling me to let go, to move on. To go live my life.

I'm not sure how long I stood there, but it was long enough to rejuvenate me. He wanted me to go forward. Nodding my head, I whispered, "I will always love you."

I made my way back to the car, asking the driver to take me to the post office because I was sure there would be stacks of mail. Yep, you guessed it. Two boxes full.

After that, I went to the real estate office I'd hired to tend to my apartment. As it turns out, the tenant is moving out at the end of the month. I made arrangements to have the place painted and redecorated. I would move back in, in two weeks' time. I was shocked when I discovered it was nearing the end of September.

So, now, I sit here in the hotel room, wondering how I should surprise the hell out of both of you. I smile, thinking about your reactions. I think I'll just show up. Well, maybe I'll call first, just to make sure you are there.

I've spent weeks going through the boxes of mail. I discovered a letter from a lawyer, telling me that I needed to contact him regarding John's will. I sat that one aside. There were a great deal of letters from people wanting to buy the winery. Not sure it's mine to sell. I decided to call the lawyer.

"Yes, can I please speak to Mr. Reynolds?"

"May I ask whose calling?" the woman said.

"Rebecca Michaels, it's in regard to a few letters he sent me concerning my husband's will."

"Please hold."

I sat there for a few minutes, holding the phone, when a man picked up. "Mrs. Michaels?"

"Yes, I've received some letters from you concerning my husband's will."

"I've been looking for you."

"I've been away. What is it that you want from me?"

"Well, Mrs. Michaels, would you be able to come to my office today? Or I could come to you. There is a great deal to discuss."

"I'm afraid you have me at a disadvantage. I wasn't aware my husband had a will."

"Yes, he did. Why don't you come over and we can sit down and discuss it?"

I looked at the clock. "I can be there shortly. I'm staying at the Seasons until tomorrow."

"That would be great. I'll see you then."

I hung up the phone, looking at it. What did John do? Why would he have a will? Wouldn't the winery go to his family? I'm confused. But I guess I'll find out.

A few more days have passed, and I am now back in my old apartment, which is new. I couldn't come back here with it looking the same as it did when I met John. The shadow of him is still here, and I still can't bring myself to sleep in the bed. Not after him, not after those two nights I spent with him.

I think I'm still in shock that he did what he did. He made me believe that he wanted something more with me, made me want something more and then just left me there. Was it a cruel joke? Did he do this to me on purpose?

I stand in the doorway of my bedroom and look at the bed. It's not John I see in it anymore, it's him. He made me feel again, and then just as he appeared in my life, he disappeared. I don't even know his last name. That's actually a bit funny because he doesn't even know my real name. I never told him. I didn't want to be Rebecca Michaels anymore. I didn't want who I was to interfere with what we were becoming.

As it turns out, John left everything to me. But his family had tried for years to find me because they wanted the winery, so I did the right thing and gave it to them. It was never mine. The only reason it held any value to me was because I shared it with them.

I did go back out there one last time to feel them again before I moved forward, before I become me again. Well, the me I am now without them. I spent the day walking around, letting the memories come to me, and I embraced them. I didn't run from them. I can't do that anymore. He was right. John wouldn't want this for me.

I've spent the last week buying new clothes, eating normal food, and just being me.

Janet, I think I'm going to come and see you today. I've been back here close to six weeks now. I've got my shit together and I think it's time we had a chat.

When I look at that number, I realize that it's been nine weeks since those two nights we spent together. Why is he still in my thoughts? Why can I still smell him, hear his laugh? Did I connect with him? It's stupid to think this way, because if I meant a damn thing to him he wouldn't have left. He wouldn't have just walked away.

Walking into your office felt weird. Things have changed—new furniture, new secretary. Your name was still on the door, Janet Plum, so I knew you were still here. I don't think you'll ever give up this job. It's in your blood.

Walking up to the desk, I whispered, "Is Janet in her office?"

The girl looked at me like I was nuts. "Who are you? Do you have an appointment?"

"I'm an old friend, and no, no appointment. Can I go in?"

"I'm sorry, but she is on a call right now with the head of a publishing company."

I smiled at her. "I'll be just a minute."

I walked past her and opened her door. The look on your face is one I will never forget. You screamed and dropped the phone You were out of your chair and had me in your arms a second later. God, girl, it was good to see you.

"Oh my God, Rebecca," you screamed.

I was laughing, I mean really laughing. I didn't realize until that moment how much I missed you.

"Where have you been?"

"Finding myself again."

"Holy shit, wait until Paula hears that you are back. Oh my God, come on in and sit down." Then you yelled out the door, "Hold all my calls and cancel my next appointment."

I walked over and sat down in the chair, and you moved behind your desk where the phone still sat there.

"Shit," you said, picking it up. "Mr. Railing, I'm so sorry. I've just had a ghost walk through the door. Can I call you back?" You had the biggest smile on your face. "Thank you."

Hanging up, you turned your full attention to me. We talked for about an hour, but I didn't tell you about this, about my writing here, and I didn't tell you about him. It doesn't matter anymore. Well, that's a lie. It matters a great deal to me.

We settled on having dinner at the Seasons later that night, and I left. I just wandered around thinking about going to see Paula, but I'm not there yet. I don't want to be pressured to write anymore. I just don't have the story in me. I thought about going to see Gus, maybe try to get my old job back. It's not that I need the money; John made sure I'll never had to work again in my life, and I still have all that money from my books and the movie deal.

Then I came home and here I am, filling my quota. It's a sorry excuse for words on the page, but I am a woman of my word and I did sign the contract.

Dinner with you, Janet, was just like I remember. You make me laugh with your energy.

"So, what's been happening in your life?" I asked.

"Jesus, what hasn't been happening? Did you know that Mr. Railing passed away about two months ago?"

I smiled. "How would I know that? I thought you were talking to him when I walked in today?"

Shaking your head, you told me, "No, that was Richard Railing, his son. He took over the publishing company when his father passed away. He's in some sort of transition period, getting it ready to hand over to his younger brother. God, wait until you meet him. He is so fucking gorgeous, but he's dating this fucking high society bitch. I can't stand her."

I giggled. "You sound like you want him for yourself."

"Shit, who wouldn't? The man is six feet of nothing but pure sexiness. But yeah, he only has eyes for the bitch. You know the kind—legs that go on forever, perfect tits, perfect teeth."

I laughed. "Yeah, I know the type. Listen, if he prefers that type of woman, then it's his loss for not seeing you. Because, frankly, you're perfect."

"Thank you. You're not so bad yourself. You look really good, Bec. I mean really good."

"Hey, what was in that box you sent me?"

"You didn't open it?" I shook my head. "It's fan mail. Hundreds of letters from your fans."

"Well, thank you, but I left it at the lake house. I wasn't in a good place. I haven't been in a good place, but I'm much better now."

We had a great time catching up, and we exchanged numbers before we left. I got a new phone. I still haven't been able to turn my old one on.

~

I've spent my time going through the boxes of mail, and I signed the winery over. His brother insisted on paying me for it. I kept telling him no, but in the end, I was tired of arguing with him. I figured, when he gets ready to rebuild, I will just pay the contractor.

I managed to pay off all the debt we had and got my credit cards reinstated. They were very understanding about what happened.

You know, I find it much easier to say the words now. To tell people that he is gone, that they are gone. I don't like all the condolences that come along with telling people, but I suppose that's how society works.

So, I'm sitting here, and my phone rings. Janet, yes it was you, all excited about a meeting with Mr. Railing.

"Oh my God, Bec, I got a call from Mr. Railing about you."

"About me? What are you talking about?"

"Well, it would seem that he wanted to know if you were going to fulfil your contract and possibly sign a new one. Also, I was approached by some movie exec. about your second book. Let me set up a meeting with Railing."

"Janet, I'm not writing anymore. I am filling the quota for the contract I signed with Paula, but I don't want another one. I'm done. I have nothing left."

"Well, he asked to see you, so I made an appointment with him tomorrow at one. We can have lunch after and talk about this movie deal."

"Fine, but I am going to tell him the same thing I just told you. I'm done."

"Whatever. I'll see you tomorrow. Same place as Paula's office, but on the fifty-fifth floor."

"That's fine, then we can stop and see Paula on our way out. Have you told her that I'm back?"

"No, actually, I haven't. I'll see you tomorrow. Be here are twelve-thirty."

So, this is where this little testament of my feelings, emotions, and all around fucked up head gets even more interesting for both of you. I can just imagine what you are saying right about now. I can see the two of you with your heads together going, 'Oh my God'.

I met you, Janet, at the publishing house, at twelve-thirty like you wanted.

We rode the elevator up past your office, Paula. I really am a bit shocked that you didn't know I was there. Strange with you being my contact person in the company and me having a meeting with your boss.

So, we were sitting in the waiting room. Well, it's not really a waiting room, but a few chairs and a couch in a very posh office. I mean, it reeked of money. High society snob money.

We were sitting looking at each other, talking, when we heard her voice, a shrill of a voice. "Oh, Richard, you make me laugh."

"I'm glad I amuse you," the voice said, and my heart literally stopped beating in my chest.

Slowly, I turned my head as my body rose from the chair, just as I watched him kiss her on the temple. His arm draped across her shoulders, and her body leaned into his.

I swear to God, I saw black spots in my vision. It was him, my Border Collie's human. As he turned his head and his eyes connected with mine, it felt like time stopped. It was so quiet; I thought I went deaf.

I was frozen to my spot as I watched his eyes change, his arm falling from her shoulder. His whole body changed. My head slightly moved back and forth, and then all hell broke loose.

"Becca?" His word was whispered, but it sounded and felt like a gun shot.

My feet were moving, propelling me toward the elevators.

"No!" he shouted.

I felt myself jump, but I didn't stop. The tears were coming, and no way was he going to see me cry. Not again, not ever again. I hit the button, praying the doors would open, but they didn't.

His arm wrapped around my waist, and he pulled me against his body. "Where have you been? I've been searching the fucking country for you."

I tried to step away from him. "Let me fucking go!" I screamed. He let me go, and I spun around. "You got what you wanted." It all made sense to me now. He was there to bring me back here, to write more fucking books for his company. "You fucking liar."

I turned around, pushing the button again.

"What are you talking about? I didn't lie about anything. Where did you go? Why did you leave?"

"I could ask you the same question, but you know what?" I turned around. "I don't fucking care!" I shouted.

His hands grabbed my face, and he kissed me. God, his kisses are to die for. But I pushed him away and slapped him across the face. "Don't ever fucking touch me again."

"No, you need to listen to me. I came back. I came back for you, but you were gone."

"Fuck you!" I screamed at him.

He opened his mouth to say something when the bitch he kissed spoke up. I hadn't even realized she was standing there. "Richard, what is going on? Who is this woman?"

"Kelly, listen, I can't do this with you. I don't want to do this with you. I only went out with you because my brother set this up. This is the woman I love, the woman I've been searching for."

I was like, what? "Oh, you love me now? Now that you know who I am. You did this. When your sister told you who I was, you played me."

"No, I love you. I loved you then. I love you now. You weren't ready to hear it. You weren't ready to feel it. You needed to heal."

"Oh, and it was your job to fix me?"

The elevator doors opened, and I turned and walked in, pushing the button for the bottom floor.

"No!" he yelled, sticking his leg in the door. "No, you aren't running from me again. No fucking way, not after what we shared."

"What we shared? We didn't share anything but a bunch of fucking lies. You're a liar!" I screamed at him.

He smiled. "Come on, get it all out."

"Fuck you!"

"Not yet, but we'll get there," he smiled.

I pushed past him back into his office and started walking. "Bec, wait up," Janet called out.

"Did you know?" I spun around to confront her. "Did you fucking know?"

"Know what? What the hell is going on?"

I could tell by the look on your face, Janet, that you didn't have a clue. He was coming after me. I could see the smile on his face. As he moved through the room, I took a few steps backward.

"I'm not done with you yet," he said and picked me up, pulling me over his shoulder. He was carrying me back to the elevator.

"Richard, what are you doing?" his girlfriend asked.

"I'm fixing my life. Becca Storm, this is Kelly Richardson. Kelly, this is my soon-to-be wife. She's been missing for the past three months."

"I'm not marrying you," I shouted. Raising my head, I looked at her. "He's all yours."

The elevator door was still open, and when he walked in, he turned and did something. "Goodbye, Kelly," he said as the doors closed.

"Put me down!"

"Not on your life, sweetheart."

The doors opened, and he started moving again. Picking my head up, I looked around. We were in an apartment. "Where are we?"

"My place."

"Where are you taking me?"

He was moving through the place.

"To the one place I know you can't get away from me."

"Oh, wait, let me guess, to your bed? Fat chance."

I had no idea what I was saying. I think all my blood was moving into my brain. I had a secret smile on my face. It felt good to be manhandled by him. I spotted Ella on the floor in the bedroom, and her head popped up and she barked as we moved through the room.

"Hi, girl," I said as the flooring changed. He shut the door and set me down. I'll admit it, I was dizzy, so I put my hands on his forearms. When my head stopped spinning, I realized we were in a bathroom. "Really?"

"It's the only room I know you can't get out of."

"What, the closet wasn't available?"

"Oh, it's available, but we aren't leaving here until you understand a few things, and I didn't want you to have to use the bathroom as an excuse to get away. When I am done, if you still want to leave, then you can leave."

I didn't want to leave. God, how I'd missed him. He still smelled like heaven. "Then get it over with because I have things to do."

He smiled. "God, you look good. Healthy. You've gained some weight. It's nice."

I gave him my evil face. "So, what, you brought me in here to sling insults at me?" I knew he wasn't; I knew what he meant. But I didn't want him to know that it felt good that he noticed.

"That morning that you left to go home, there were several messages on my phone from my sister and my brother. Our father had a heart attack. I didn't even think about it; I just got in my car and left. I didn't think about leaving you a note until I was halfway back here. I couldn't call you and tell you because you don't have a phone."

Yes, before you even think it, I feel like an ass.

"He passed away eight days after I got here. It was three weeks before I could make it back to the lake house. When I got back there, you were gone. I waited for you for a week and you never came back. I had so much shit to do back here, so I left you a note, telling you where I was and begging you to come. I didn't want to leave you, Becca. I didn't. But it was my father."

I felt the tears coming. "I'm sorry for what you went through. I'm sorry I was being a bitch to you."

He shook his head. "You have every right to be. What we shared was something big for you. I know that, and I just walked away from it, from you, with no regard for how you felt. I am so sorry for doing that to you. Just as you were starting to come around, I just left."

"It hurt, yes, but everything we talked about made me realize you were right. I needed to start living again. So, I came back here, where my life was, before John."

"I went out to the vineyard a few times, hoping you would show up there. I couldn't... no, I can't imagine what you have been through."

Just then I remembered the girl he was kissing and got pissed again. He wasn't getting away with this shit. "Who was that woman?"

He chuckled. I'm glad he found it funny. "A replica of my wife. My brother thought it was time for me to move on. She is a friend of his and his wife,"

"She seems perfect for you. Now that I've heard what you had to say, can I leave? I left my friend downstairs, and I have lunch plans."

"No, you don't."

"What? Are you going to keep me hostage here?"

"Fucking right I am." He stepped forward. "You're not leaving again. I'm not letting you go. Why didn't you tell me your real name?"

I stood my ground, squaring my shoulders. "Because, at that time, Rebecca Michaels was dead inside. She couldn't function."

"And now, she's here alive in our bathroom?"

I shook my head. "Our bathroom?"

He nodded, moving forward another step. "Yes, our bathroom. Or, at least, it will be ours until I finish this transition for my brother, and then we are going back to the lake. I want no part of this world, of these people."

"What makes you think I want anything to do with you?"

His hand came up and touched my face. "I was in that bed, too. I know what I felt," he said in his sexy ass voice. Damn it, I knew I was going to give in.

"What does that even mean?"

His thumb dragged across my bottom lip. "You are so beautiful. So fucking sexy and you don't even know it. The way you touch me, the way you kiss me, I know what I felt."

I swallowed hard as he moved into my personal space. Who is this man, and why does he affect me like this?

"It was nothing. I was just horny, alone, tired of being scared."

"Like now?"

His mouth came down on mine. I pulled my head back, but his fingers wrapped around my neck. "No, not now."

"Liar," he whispered on my lips as he kissed me.

I knew my body was going to betray my words. This man's kisses are too much for any one woman. He made my toes curl. Yes, I kissed him back, the bastard. He knows all right. He fucking knows.

I pushed him away. "You're with someone else." I moved away from him.

"No, I'm not. You heard what I said to her."

"But you kissed her. You've slept with her."

Shaking his head, he denied it. "No, on both counts. Really, you think I'm that shallow, that I would want a woman who wears far too much makeup and horrible lipstick? A woman who has fake tits? No, not my type."

"Oh, and I'm your type?"

"In every possible way."

He reached out, pulling me to him. I wanted to fight him, but I didn't. He felt so damn good. When he kissed me again, I kissed him back. He lifted me up and wrapped my legs around him. Somehow, he managed to open the door and we ended up on his bed.

As he laid me on the bed, he looked at me and said, "You're mine now. You are mine. I've waited my whole life for you."

I mean, come on. Who doesn't want to hear shit like that?

"No, I'm not yours. I belong to me."

He chuckled. "No, you're mine. I love you."

"You're not the boss of me," I mumbled as he kissed my neck.

"I don't want to be the boss of you, I want to love you. I want to spend my life with you. I thanked your husband while I was out there. I thanked him for loving you, for treating you so well. I also told him that I have a high standard to live up to, and trust me, I don't ever plan on stopping. You're mine."

Our kiss lasted a long time, a very long time. I admit it, I got lost in him. Completely lost in him. When we finally separated, I realized he still had his suit on. I still had my shoes on. Pushing on his chest, he moved off of me, but he wasn't really laying on me. I got up and walked out of his room. I needed to clear my head.

Walking into the living room, I just stood there looking out the window. I happened to notice a pillow and blanket on the floor. A small smile came across my lips. He still sleeps on the couch.

When he came out, he was missing his shoes, socks, tie and jacket. Walking up behind me, he wrapped his arms around me. "Talk to me."

"When you didn't come back, I nearly thought you were just a figment of my imagination. I was scared I was going insane. But instead of hiding, cowering in the darkness like I have for so long, I got pissed off. Not sure if it was at you or me. Me for thinking you were real, or you for being real and then leaving me like you did."

"I'm so sorry. I can't take it back, and I can't change it. I think that, even if I could, I wouldn't. I realized when I went back there and you weren't there, that I love you. I felt it here." His hand came up and rested on my heart. "I don't want you to leave. I want you to stay. Will you stay with me?"

Yes, bitches, I stayed.

Turning in his arms, my fingers unbuttoned his shirt so I could see his chest. "I felt it here when I realized you left me." I put my hand on his chest. Tilting my head up, I felt brave. "Don't leave me again."

"I have another month until I hand this company over to my brother. Will you go back to the lake with me and live life with me?"

"I just redecorated my apartment."

"Then we can stay there. I don't care. I just know that I have been crazy these past few months looking for you, and you just walk right into my office and there you are."

I nodded; I didn't care. He was here, and I was here. We were together. We stood by the window kissing. "Come to bed with me," he whispered.

I so wanted to. "Yes," was all I got out of my mouth before he had me wrapped around him, and we were moving.

"Ella, living room," he said. When she ran out, he shut the door with his foot. Walking to the bed, he laid me down and took off my boots.

Smiling, he pulled my pants off. I watched as he dropped his shirt on the floor. Then he undid his slacks and they fell to the floor. He looked fucking marvelous, ladies, and I mean fucking marvelous. My God, my heart was slamming in my chest when he put his knee between my legs and then his hands on either side of my head.

"I don't have any condoms," he whispered on my lips.

"Okay," I whispered back.

So, no sex, you perverts. I'm smiling right now. I'm not on the pill, and I certainly do not want a child. No fucking way.

He pulled off my shirt, and we got under the covers and laid in bed, kissing and talking and touching one another. His hands are so soft, but we needed to learn about each other. We spent eighteen hours talking, kissing, eating, and sleeping.

To say it was anything other than what it was wouldn't be right. He is very careful with me, and it's something that I think I need right now. He's right; we don't know each other at all. I don't know if I love him, but he sure makes my heart flutter.

My heart, the cold stone in my chest that beat for one man and my children. I was a little confused when he said he went out to the winery. How did he know about the winery? If he knew about it, then he knew my real name.

I wanted to ask him, but I didn't want to end what we had been sharing. But if I didn't know the truth, then wouldn't that have us starting out again as a lie? So, I asked him as we sat eating our breakfast.

"You said you went out to the winery."

"Yes."

"How did you know to go there?"

"I remember my sister telling me what happened to you. So, when I couldn't find you, I searched the internet for the story. It was horrific. I knew you had lost your husband and children, and there was only one place that had happened. I assumed that was it."

"Well, if you knew Johnathan's name was Michaels, wouldn't you have known mine was?"

To be honest, my heart was slamming in my chest. I wanted him to say the right thing. I wanted, no want this to be real.

"Many women, especially professional women, don't take their husband's last names. When I searched, or had the investigator search for you, I couldn't find one Becca Michaels. It never dawned on me that your name was Rebecca." I nodded at him. It made sense. "Hey," he said softly, getting off his chair to kneel on the floor next to me. "I'm not playing a game. I want this with you. I want a relationship with you. I want to love you. Hell, I love you. Believe that, okay?"

I smiled at him. Who wouldn't? You've both seen him, right?

"So, you made a promise to my dead husband to love me better than he did?"

He chuckled. "Sort of. I don't think I can love you better than he did. But I can love you differently. I can and will and do love you my way. I just hope I can make you smile like you are right now for the rest of your life."

I laughed "You are very confident that you're going to be around that long."

"Listen, sweetheart, I'm not going anywhere anytime soon. I will stalk you if you don't love me back."

I laughed. "We shall see."

To be honest, I think I already do. But we shall see. Right now, I am coming down from an eighteen-hour high. I need to think and breathe. I liked that we were at the lake without interruptions.

Without this life invading my thoughts. Here, I have relationships I need to mend. I have more here, and I'm not so sure I want more. As miserable as life was for me there, I also healed there. We shall see.

We finished our meal and then we left his penthouse apartment. It's not my taste, but it's a very nice place.

When the elevator stopped on his floor, he pinned me against the wall and kissed me stupid. "Don't leave," he whispered. "Promise me you won't leave."

"I won't leave. I told you I just redecorated my apartment. Do you have a phone?"

Smiling, he pulled it out of his pocket and handed it to me. I dialed my number, and my phone rang in my bag. His smile got bigger.

"Now, you have my number."

"I'll call you when I get done today. Can Ella come to your house?"

I laughed. Yes, I laughed. "I have a yard. It's more of a townhouse. Yes, she can come to my house."

"Good, because I hate that apartment."

Someone cleared their throat, and he wiggled his eyebrows at me. Turning, his secretary was standing there.

"Jackie, this is Becca Michaels."

"Yes, sir, I know Mrs. Michaels."

"Good, she has open-door access. No matter what I am doing, she gets in."

"Understood. Sir, your brother is in your office, and he isn't happy."

"When is Alexander happy?" Turning to me, he said, "I'll see you later on."

I smiled. "Go, work. I have to go see Janet. Oh, and I'm not writing anymore, so don't worry about a contract. But yes, I will finish out my other one."

"Good to know."

Then he turned and walked out of the elevator. I leaned against the wall and let my breath out. Jesus, Mary, mother of God.

~

I didn't stop and see you, Janet, and for that I am sorry. You're so cute blowing up my phone. Yes, there is a great deal we need to talk about, but to be honest with you, I don't want to talk about him. Not yet anyway.

I don't even know what to make of all this. He said just about everything a man could say to a woman. He even said, 'I love you', and no, I didn't say it back, because I'm not so sure that I do. I'm still fighting with myself on how not to love John anymore, how not to be in love with him. He is everything, my everything. Well, he was my everything.

When I went back out to the winery, there were two separate work crews. His brother had already started to rebuild. As I walked the vineyard, I remembered the many strolls we had through the vines. I sat down on the earth where we made love, and I cried. I'm a mess. I stood in the living room, or, at least, what I think was the living room, and watched the memories of my family in my mind.

How am I supposed to let any of this go? I'm not sure I can. Do I have enough room in my heart to love Rick? Do I want to love him? He seemed so attached to that woman. What was her name? Oh yeah, Kelly. It feels as if he didn't waste any time moving on from me, not that there was a me and him. Why couldn't he find me? I'm still a bit concerned about this.

Paula, you know my name, and if he really wanted to find me, why didn't he ask you or Janet?

I think I need to figure that out before I move any further into this. I'm not sure this is the healthiest thing for me. I should get on my feet first before I start again. Hell, I'm not even sure I want to start again.

He helped me, but I can't assume that he is my next step just because he helped me. Isn't there some kind of syndrome for that?

Paula, I'm on my way to see you, so be ready.

I'm smiling as I write this. Paula, you crack me up.

I didn't wait for your secretary to tell you I was there. I just walked in.

"Hey, bitch!" I said.

The way your head lifted and then the shock on your face. "Oh my fucking God. What the fuck?"

I laughed. "Miss me?"

"Becca, while I live and breathe. Where's my book, bitch?" you asked as you grabbed me in your arms laughing.

It was so good to see you. We sat and had a great chat, all the way up until...

"I'm about halfway through it."

"When can I read some pages?"

"Yeah, that's just it. You can't. Paula, when I turn it in, there are no revisions. I want you to print it just the way it is. Make sure the spelling and everything is correct but don't change a thing."

"I promise, I won't. So, tell me about yesterday."

"What are you talking about?"

"Well, Kelly is a friend of mine. We set her up with Alex's brother..."

"Wait, Alex is his brother?" You nodded. "Are you fucking kidding me? He fucking knew how to find me. He knew who I was?"

"What are you talking about? How do you know Richard?"

I stood up, furious. Looking at you, I said on my way out the door, "I don't know Richard, I know Rick. I've gotta go. I'm not signing another contract, and when I finish the book, I'm done." I opened the door and walked out.

I hit the button for the fifty-fifth floor in the elevator so hard I hurt my finger. When the doors opened, I was moving. I didn't stop to say hi to his secretary; I just walked into his office. I didn't really walk. I stormed in, slamming the door open.

"Are you fucking serious? Your brother is married to Paula, my publisher, and you couldn't fucking find me? You are so full of shit. And what the hell? If you say you loved me, would it fucking matter if you used a condom or not? I was right."

He stood up when I walked in. He was sitting in a chair by the couch. To be honest, I didn't see anyone else in the room.

"You fucking knew who I was from the very beginning. You only did what you did so I would come back to reality to fulfill a fucking contract, so I could sign a new one. Well, you know what? You can go fuck yourself. I quit. I fucking quit two and half years ago. But now, I really fucking quit. Take me to court and sue me for breach of contract, because I'm done. I'm pretty sure I can turn this last book over to any fucking publishing company in the country."

I went to turn to leave, and he grabbed me around the waist, pulling me against him. "No, I am not letting you go."

I struggled to get away from him. "Let me go, Rick. I want no part of you. I don't do liars. You took from me, and I got nothing but lies and deceit for it. Let me the fuck go."

"I won't. I was there, too I was in that bed, too. I was on that beach with you. I know what I felt. I didn't lie to you. I've never lied to you."

With his breath hot on my neck, my body was tingling.

"Failure to tell the truth is a lie."

"I can say the same for you. You didn't tell me who you were."

"Fuck you. I am Becca Storm. Your own sister told you that. You knew his name, and you knew my name. Let me go, Rick. Let me the fuck go."

I felt his arm slack, and my heart broke. I think I wanted him to fight for me, and it pissed me off even more that he was going to just let me go.

"I said I didn't have a condom because I'm not sure you're ready for that yet. Hell, I fucking know I'm not. I just want us. I want us just the way we've been. I need to know you are in this with me. I fucking love you."

The tears were coming. "You don't fucking love me. You don't even know me."

"Hence the no sex. But if that's the issue here, the fact that I haven't made a move on you, well, let's go. I will rectify that right now."

"No, it isn't going to happen. Not now, not ever."

I was shocked when he spun me around and picked me up. He walked us to a wall or door and leaned into me. His hands grabbed my face. "I fucking love you," he said softly and kissed me.

I fought him, but not really. His kisses, ladies, are to die for, at least they are for me.

His hands moved into my hair as he deepened the kiss. When we pulled apart, he whispered, "I'm not letting you go. I feel you. I feel how you feel, and I'm not walking away from that. Not now, not next week, not next year."

The tears fell from my eyes. "You lied to me."

Shaking his head, his thumbs wiped at my tears. "Don't cry, beautiful. I didn't lie to you." And yeah, he kissed me again. It was the clearing of a throat that pulled him back. "Fuck," he whispered.

I looked over his shoulder to see Alex and that woman Kelly standing there watching us. "Fuck," I whispered.

He chuckled, my eyes looking into his. "Exactly."

"Put me down."

"No, you're not going to run from me. I won't let you."

"You're not the boss of me."

He busted out laughing and stepped back, letting me go. I fixed my clothes, and he turned around. "Alex, I believe you know Becca. Kelly."

I swear, if looks could kill, I would be dead by both of them.

Paula, I'm not so sure your husband cares too much for me right now. Oh well.

"Richard, what the hell is going on? Becca," Alex nodded to me.

"Well, brother, I'm in love with this woman, and I'm hoping one day she will marry me."

"I told you, I'm not marrying you. You're going to be lucky if I ever talk to you again. I've said what I needed to say to you, so I'm leaving."

"No, you're not leaving. I told you last night, I am not letting you go. I know how you feel."

I shook my head. "You're a liar and you used me to get what you wanted."

"You slept with her?" Kelly said.

I nearly busted out laughing when he looked right at her and said, "Not yet, but I'm hopeful."

"We are going out. You told me you wanted to see where this was going. That's what I'm doing here." She turned to Alex. "You said he wanted me. I'm going to be humiliated." Back to Rick. "You've taken me all over this town and introduced me as your girlfriend."

I watched him shake his head. "No, that's not true. I introduced you as my date, and that's what you were, my date."

"It implies girlfriend, Richard. Becca is not the woman you need to align yourself with." Alex looked at me. "No offense, Becca. You know I like you."

I smiled at him. "No, Alex, I know you don't like me, and I know you are the reason why Paula never tried to find me. The only thing I ever was to you was a payday. You only tolerate my friendship with your wife because of the millions of dollars I brought to this company. Well, you don't have to worry about that anymore. I quit."

"I'm sorry you feel that way. Our lawyers will be in touch."

"No, they won't," Rick said to him. "I quit, too. You want a transition, well, you figure it out, little brother. I'm done. I left this shit business a long time ago."

"Because you had to recover from the loss of your wife. But now you're back."

He made me jump when he busted out laughing. "Let me tell you, little brother, Kelly is not an option for me. I let you bulldoze me into marrying Julia, but not again. That bitch cheated on me every chance she had. I'm done."

"Oh, and you think she can love you? You are living in a dream world. Life sucks, and if you think you are ever going to find a relationship that is true, you really are nuts. Who the hell stays faithful to the same person for life?"

I couldn't let this one go. "Alex, are you saying you're not faithful to your wife?"

He just stood there looking at me.

I'm sorry, Paula, but your husband is a fucking cheater.

"My wife understands what's at stake here."

I smiled. "What's at stake here? Her job? Her livelihood? What, Alex?"

Rick turned to me. "Come on. Let's go get Ella and get the hell out of here."

I laughed. "So sure of yourself, aren't you? What makes you think I want this with you?"

"This," he said. Grabbing my face, he kissed me.

I pulled away. "Stop doing that."

"Becca, will you excuse us, please? We were in the middle of a marriage negotiation," Alex said.

"Not a problem." I turned to walk out the door, when he stopped me.

Yes, Paula, your husband is trying to negotiate a marriage of your friend to your brother-in-law. I know you know that.

Looking at his brother, he said, "I already told you I'm not doing this."

"But father's will was specific. In order to inherit the company, you have to marry. Kelly is the choice."

"You forget one thing here, brother. I don't want the company. Wait a minute, you knew who Becca was, and you knew I was looking for her. You set me up? You fucking set me up. Fuck, did you pay the P.I. to not find her?" Alex didn't say anything. "You did. I told you I was only doing this to help you out. But you had this planned all along. Oh my God." Looking at Kelly, he said, "I wouldn't marry you if you were the last woman on the planet. You wear far too much makeup, your perfume makes me sick, and I will not fuck another woman with fake tits. You are so not my type."

Alex looked at me. "And her tits are real?"

Really? My tits? How the hell did my tits get into a conversation? What the fuck?

"Excuse me," I said. "My tits are not up for discussion. I really need to leave."

I turned and opened the door, and his sister, Alice, I think her name is, was standing there. "Becca Storm, I heard you were in town. Why?"

I just stood there looking at her. "You people are fucked up. I have to go." Turning, I looked at Alex. "Good luck finding me." And I walked out. I didn't have to wait for the elevator because the door was open. I could see his face when I pushed the button to go down. He looked like a lost little boy. I felt bad for him. I really did, but there was no way I was staying there.

Paula, you live a fucked up life with a very fucked up man. If you even think this way of living is acceptable, there is something terribly wrong with you. I'm sorry, but you will read these pages, like, never. I will finish it just because I am a woman of my word, but you won't ever get it. No one will. I think I'm in shock.

He's called me eighteen times, and I haven't answered my phone. I'm pretty sure he has left messages, as well. It's been three days since that bullshit at his office went down. I so miss the peace and quiet of my lake house.

As I sit here and look around this place, it makes me sad to know that I am leaving it again. Only this time, I am not going back into the darkness. I am just going back to my lake house and not ever leaving. I prefer the solitude it provides. You people are all fucking nuts. It makes me wonder if John felt the same way. If the reasons why he pushed me was so he could indulge in this 'cheat on your wife' thing.

What Alex said to me, that thing about 'how is anyone expected to stay faithful to just one person', is messed up. Seriously?

Paula, do you cheat on your husband? I understand now why you never came to see me. It's good to know that the only thing I was to you was a paycheck. Deceit. That's all this place is.

I will be back to this. I have a doctor's appointment.

You'll be happy to know that I am healthy as a horse. I never really understood that saying. Anyway, I stopped and talked to the real estate agent who handled my sub-lease, and I am putting this town-house on the market. This place is not for me anymore. I'm too old for this shit, for this game playing.

I met a man at the downfall of my life. If I hadn't met him, I think I might have died out there. But I have to thank him for coming into my life when I needed him. So, thank you, Rick, and then no thank you for anything you might think in your mind I want.

Why would I walk away from a gorgeous man who obviously wants me? I know you are all wondering. Well, to you, it might not be obvious, but you weren't in that room. I mean, I'm a writer, but to describe the tense emotions that took place in there is nearly impossible.

I'm still a little miffed as to why he would defy his brother, but when his sister walked in, he froze. He didn't follow me out. Something just isn't right. Why would his brother stop a private investigator from giving him knowledge about me? These are questions I want the answers to. I wonder who the P.I. was? It doesn't really matter.

My bags are packed, and I even took the time to buy some heavier clothes. I'm going back to my lake house, and I am going to get fat and finish this book and be done with it. Maybe I'll get cable television and just veg out on nothing.

I think I've come full circle. I've grieved, and yes, I'm still holding on to my anger, but it's a different kind of anger. Going back to the winery helped a great deal. My memories came back, and I settled. Time to move on. Time to go.

Someone is knocking on my door. God, please, don't let it be him.

Now, I think I have heard and seen everything, and you know what? Society is fucked. I mean, super really fucked.

That was Alice. Yep, you guess it, Rick's sister. She came over to give me a heads up. You ready for this? I'm not. I wasn't when it happened a few hours ago, and I'm not now.

I opened the door, and she was standing there looking like she just literally swallowed the canary.

"Can I help you?" I asked.

"Becca Storm, can I come in? I think it's time we had a talk."

"It's Rebecca Michaels, and yeah, that's probably not a good idea."

"Nonsense, let's have a chat."

She actually pushed her way past me into my townhouse. She made me laugh when she turned her nose up.

"What do you want?" Yep, I was being rude.

"My brother, Alex, told me what was going on between you and Richard. I'm here to find out if you had sex with him."

I laughed. "That really is none of your business."

"But it is. I'm here to make sure you understand what happens if you conceive a child with him."

"What does or does not happened between your brother and myself is none of your business."

"If he conceives a child with someone who is not of proper breeding, then that child can never inherit the family company. He is the oldest sibling, so his child will inherit. It's the way it's been for generations. My children, nor Alex's have that birthright. Probably why neither one of us have children. We are willing to pay you a substantial amount of money to just disappear. He seems to think he is in love with you. I personally don't see it. You have no real breeding, no bloodline to speak of."

I just stood there, wondering if I heard her right? I was so curious, I had to ask.

"How much?"

She looked at me. "Twenty-five million."

I nearly stroked out right there. Then it happened. I couldn't stop it, I couldn't control it. I laughed, and I mean I laughed. It was long, and the look on her face just made me laugh more.

Finally, I was able to form coherent words. "You're serious?" She nodded. "Please, leave my house and don't ever come back here. I didn't have sex with your brother, and I don't have any intentions on having sex with your brother." I walked to the door. "Get out."

She stood there for a few minutes looking at me, and then she just left. I've been sitting on the couch in shock. What the fuck was that? Seriously? I have to go.

CHAPTER TEN

It's been about a week since I've been back here. The ghosts are all around me. I can't believe I just left my life again. But it's not really my life anymore. The people I surrounded myself with are not the people I believed them to be.

It's funny how isolation brings out your spidey senses. I would have never imagined that both Janet and Paula were just cogs in a machine. A fucked up machine, but a machine none the less.

I thought that people who removed themselves from society were nuts, that they had emotional problems or were just hard on their luck, but I totally understand it now. After years of being here, and healing here, I can't, nor do I want to live in that world.

I can't stop thinking about him and the struggle he is fighting. I found his note. I think I want him to be down the beach right now. He did come back for me; I was just too impatient to wait for him. But I'm here now, and I have no intentions on leaving.

I can't help but wonder why he didn't follow me out, why he just let me leave. I can think of a hundred different reasons. Maybe he knew I should leave while he fought them. Maybe he thought I couldn't handle it. Maybe he didn't really want me, or maybe he was just defying his family by wanting me. Who knows? I could spend a lifetime trying to figure it out. But in all reality, I'm not really sure I care why he just let me go.

Weeks have passed, and summer here is coming to an end. His month is over, and he isn't coming. I suppose, deep down inside, I wished it. I think I might have even wanted it. I'll admit it, I want him. But I wanted my husband and my children, and we all know that didn't happen. He's probably married by now to that horrible woman Kelly. I feel bad for him if he is, and I pray that he doesn't kiss her the way he kissed me, or touch her the way he touched me.

There really isn't anything I can do about it but put him away, just like I have John and the children.

On a good note, I've been cooking and eating like I should. Although, I'm sad, I'm not devastated like I was before. I can't let my almost feelings for him take me into the darkness. We didn't have very much time together, and the time we did have wasn't enough to send me spiraling into the abyss.

My walks on the beach will soon come to an end and planting my ass on the deck for the winter will soon be in full swing. But it still looms in the back of my mind. Why?

More time spent with my own thoughts. The weather has changed, and I'm sure that, soon, the snow will come. Why, is still the thought.

I felt connected to him in a way. Maybe it was because he pulled me out of the darkness. Perhaps he is what people call the rebound man. Maybe that's what I was to him, as well. The stepping stone to feeling again. But we did have a connection, or was it just in my mind? Was it just something I needed? An excuse?

I shouldn't have run. I should have fought for him. I should have let him know that I felt the same way. It's too late now. A marriage contract was written up to produce an heir. The things people do for money. Ridiculous.

~

I was right, the snow is here. That means the roads will be closing soon. So, I'm off to the store. I managed to get a deep freeze so I can handle this winter. Last winter, I was surviving on, well, nothing really. Be back later to finish.

I'm nearing thirty-eight thousand words, Paula. Soon, it will be finished.

I don't know why I think that is going to be a wonderful thing. These pages have become my salvation in a sense. If it wasn't for Janet giving me this stupid machine, I might not be here anymore. I may have just ended my life.

~

Now, that was exhausting. Being in a healthy state of mind is exhausting. I chuckle. The butcher was shocked to see me buying meat, and did I buy meat. I need to settle in for this long winter.

I realized today that I still haven't slept in a bed. The only time was with him. I wonder if he is sleeping in bed with her. Okay, this is getting crazy, this obsession I seem to have with him. I need to put him away, out of my mind. He isn't coming, and if he was, he would have been here already. It's been months, and he said he had only about a month left to do whatever it was he had to do.

He isn't coming for me.

He isn't coming for me.

He isn't coming for me.

Yes, I'm chanting it. I need to pull myself out of this mindset and just move on. I'm sure my thoughts can amount to more than him. I'm a fucking New York Times best seller. My imagination runs far deeper than this, than him.

Trust me, I can imagine a great deal when it comes to him. Unlike my memories of John, I can still feel Rick's lips on mine. I'm sure, with time, as with John, they will fade. Maybe the abyss of darkness is the way to go. At least, time has no meaning in the darkness. Out here in the light, it drags on and on.

I can feel, in the pit of my heart, the feeling of distraught loneliness. I should just be thankful I had the little time with him that I had. Can you fall in love with someone in such a short time? I mean, you hear of love at first sight; could this be that?

He isn't coming for me.

He isn't coming for me.

He isn't coming for me.

The snow is continual. I wonder if this is lake effect snow? To be honest, I'm not sure how big this lake is. Oh well. I still can't get him out of my mind. I haven't looked at his messages, nor have I listened to them. My phone is right here, but it's been off since that day in his office.

I should have fought for him. It doesn't matter, it doesn't.

I've decided to open the box Janet sent me, and yes, it's filled with fan mail. I'm at a place where I can read them now. Most of them are condolences. I have piles of letters.

To all of you who have written to me, thank you, from the bottom of my heart. It means a great deal to know that you all cared enough to do this.

But now that the years have passed, I am all but forgotten, even by him.

He isn't coming for me.

He isn't coming for me.

He just isn't coming for me.

Winter is in full force here at the lake. I've been secretly wishing for that imaginary lake monster to be real. The snow is huge. I can just see the top of my car. I know he isn't coming. How could he? He wouldn't be able to get through.

I really need to get a grip on reality here. I spent over two years wishing to be dead because I missed them so much. I was literally killing myself. Now, I have managed to isolate myself again, because of him. Because I think I've fallen in love with a man who is so obviously controlled by his family and so obviously unattainable to me. How pathetic is my life? How pathetic am I?

I was in my usual spot, asleep on the couch, when a weird scratching noise woke me. It was weird, after all this time to hear a woodland creature trying to get inside. I don't blame it. There's a great deal of snow out there. I wouldn't want to stay out in this mess, either. I got up and made some tea, and now I sit here, thinking. What the fuck do I have to say? There isn't much more to say, except to whine about how lonely I am, how much my heart hurts, and how much of a fool I was to think he really wanted me.

I got up to put on my UGG boots and grab my blanket to go sit on the deck. I like the bitter cold air. It smells so delicious. When I opened my door, the snow had been disturbed. Apparently, the animal that wanted in my house was rather large, leaving its paw prints all over the place. As I looked around, I could see its imprints going down what should be the stairs, and around to the car, then out into the road.

God, I was a bit freaked out; I still am. It was a pretty big animal. I hope it wasn't a bear, or a mountain lion. I don't have a gun. I will admit I'm a bit more than freaked out. But hey, at this point in the game, I really don't care what happens to me. Maybe death is an option.

I tried, John. I tried to make life work. I even went so far as to possibly fall in love with someone who didn't want me, who just used me to fulfill a contract. Maybe now it's time to believe that there is no life after death.

～

Okay, so, shit has happened since I sat here last. Shit, I am still having a hard time comprehending.

Paula, Janet, you might not believe this. I still don't.

I was sleeping, my usual mode of life these days, as with the past. I wanted him to come to me in my dreams. The darkness is the only thing I see. Who sleeps this much and never dreams? Is that even possible?

Anyway, the scratching happened again. This time, I was up and at the door in no time at all. I wasn't sure if I should open the door and scare the shit out of the unknown creature, but then I thought twice about it, because I'm not real sure how a bear would react to a tiny human screaming at him. So, I carefully moved the drapes to see what it was, and my heart stopped.

I couldn't move fast enough, ripping open my door. She was here. My Border Collie friend, she was here. She came flying in the house, knocking me on the floor and climbing on top of me, licking my face.

I hugged her. "Oh my God. Why are you here?" I asked.

Then I heard him. "She came with me."

The tears came, and I couldn't stop them. I didn't even move. I just hung on to her and cried. I don't know how I ended up in his arms, but I did. He felt so good.

"I'm sorry it took me so long to get here," he whispered in my hair.

I just nodded; it was all I could do. Ella jumped around and barked, dancing on the floor. He held on to me as tight as I hung on to him. The door was open, the room flooding with the freezing cold air, but I didn't care. He was here.

When I finally pulled back, his hands came to my face, wiping my tears. "I told you that I love you and I want this with you. I'm so sorry it took so long."

I shook my head as he kissed me. It was like nothing I'd ever known. He pulled back and got up, shutting the door and taking off his boots and coat. I just laid on the floor watching him. Was I dreaming? Am I just imagining this? He stepped toward me, stopping when he looked at the couch, and smiled. Bending down, the man picked me up like I was a bag of potatoes and carried me into the bedroom, lying me on the bed. He proceeded to remove his clothing, everything except his boxers.

I'm sorry, ladies, but the man is magnificent to look at. He pulled off my boots and my sweats. Then he pulled me up and lifted my sweatshirt off. I didn't have a bra on. When he tossed my shirt on the floor and looked at me, his eyes watered.

"God, woman, you are going to make it very difficult not to make love to you. Fucking spectacular," he sweetly moaned as he leaned in and kissed me.

We got lost in each other for hours it felt. We didn't talk, just kissed and held one another. We managed to get under the covers, and sleep sucked us both under; although, sleep is the last thing I wanted. Yes, I wanted him. I wanted all of him. But this sleep was different.

With his body behind mine, wrapped around me, it was so comforting. I don't care who you are out there in the world, sleeping in a bed is so much better than sleeping on a couch.

I woke to feel his lips on my shoulder, then he pressed me onto my stomach and kissed every inch of my back all the way to my ass. God, I wanted him. When his fingers brushed over my panties, I was a bit embarrassed that I was so wet, and I was. So wet, and so wanton of him. When he finished torturing me, I pushed up and rolled over, his lips landing on my stomach.

Yes, I did the arching of the back. I had no control. I was coming, and it felt fucking fantastic. I haven't had an orgasm in nearly three years. He slid his arm under my back, pulling my chest to his mouth. I'm not a very verbal woman when it comes to sex, but fuck if I didn't cry out when his lips wrapped around my nipple. I mean, Jesus, it was so hard. His teeth grazed it, and he nipped me. My whole body shattered just as his mouth covered mine.

I wanted this man. I managed to make my brain work, and my hands pushed his boxers down enough to free him. He was big, and hard. His cock landed on me, and I swear I came again. He grabbed the side of my panties and ripped them off me, his mouth never leaving mine as I wrapped myself around him.

He was slow pushing himself inside of me, and thank God for that, because the man was huge. Too big. He knew it, too. He filled me and then stopped, waiting for my body to adjust to him.

My God, my eyes are rolling in my head right now as I write this, just remembering the feel of him. I swear, my panties are soaked. If ever in this life you have the opportunity to have sex with a man who has a huge cock, I suggest you do. You will never be the same after that.

We made love for a very long time. I don't know how he stayed hard for so long. I know he had two orgasms. Me, well, yeah, I lost track after five. When it was over, he wouldn't let me go.

Looking up at him, my hand on his face, I whispered, "I love you."

"I know," he whispered back. "I love you. Marry me."

I shook my head. "No, I can't."

He chuckled. "Yes, you can. This is where I belong. I've always belonged here. You are mine, and I plan on keeping you for the rest of my life."

I mean, come on, fucking swoon worthy. Am I right?

I laughed, rolling away from him to use the bathroom to clean myself up. "We didn't use a condom." I was being a smart ass.

He grabbed me, pulling me back into the bed. "Oh, I know we didn't, and I don't fucking care, do you?"

I shook my head, kissing him. I felt bad, and as I sit here writing this, I feel bad. I don't have the heart to tell him that I got a shot, just in case he came. I'm good for at least three months. But I am not ever having another child.

We made love like six more times, and each time was better than the time before. We haven't really had a chance to talk about what happened and why, but I suppose it doesn't really matter. I know it does, and I know, if I'm not prepared, it is going to come and bite me in the ass.

He went back to his house to pack his clothes. He invited himself to move in here with me. Nope, not arguing with him. Not at all.

We had the chance to talk after we went another round. I don't think I had this much love and attention the first six months of my relationship with John. This man is a machine, a fucking sex machine, and he is mine. I want to giggle, just thinking about the face you are making. I'm not one for talking about my personal life, not like this, not with these very intimate details.

We were lying on the couch, him in his boxers, me in his shirt. He was at one end, and I was at the other.

"So, what happened? Did you marry Kelly?" I had to chuckle.

"There is no way I was going to marry that woman. If I had known what they were up to, I would have never taken her out."

"What happened?"

"My father's will, and his mental view point of high society. We were all raised in the most proper schools. My sister went to finishing school. We were all groomed a certain way, the way of the very rich and elite, I suppose. When my father died, his will had set into play a very barbaric way of life. Please, don't take this the wrong way. I loved my wife, very much, but when he died, I found out that it was an arranged marriage. Once it was done, it could never be undone. So, I could never have divorced her."

"Seems a bit extreme."

"You don't know the half of it. She knew of the arrangement; her requirement was to produce an heir for me, and then she could walk away with a hundred million dollars."

"Are you serious?"

"Very. Apparently, the same offer was made to Kelly, by my father, when my wife died. Well, when I came up here, they didn't know what to do when I sold everything. So, my father had his will changed, which made it near impossible for me to walk away again. No one saw you coming. No one saw me falling in love with you. My brother paid off the P.I. that I hired to lie to me and feed him the information instead. That's why Paula dropped your contract. They didn't want you to come back, especially after you saved me. They knew we had met."

"I don't understand. No one knew what was between us."

"But they did. When they were at my house at Christmas, when you came over to return the gift I had given you, remember?" I nodded. "Well, my brother bugged my house after that."

"Seriously?"

He nodded. "They knew everything; well, nearly everything. You leaving here, they didn't expect. It wasn't until Janet called Paula and told her you were back in San Francisco that they started to freak out. You being out in the waiting area of my office that day was not by coincidence. It was planned. You were supposed to see me with Kelly. They were banking on you still being messed up over your family. I guess we shocked the hell out of them when what happened, happened."

I'm shocked that you people could do something so horrible. What the fuck.

"So, that would explain your sister knowing where I live and coming over to my house."

"Seriously, she did that?"

I laughed. "Oh yeah, she wanted confirmation that we had sex. She said something about me getting pregnant and the baby not being able to inherit. I busted out laughing and asked her to leave."

He sat up. "I'm so sorry."

"It all makes sense now. How did you get out of this marriage thing with plastic Kelly?"

He laughed. "I like that. She was plastic, her boobs, her teeth. God, just thinking about her gives me the chills. Dumb as a box of rocks, but she comes from good stock, as my brother would say."

I couldn't help it; I busted out laughing. "How sad, this is all so sad. I'm sorry for what they did to you. So, how did you get out of it?"

"Well, I took my father's will and went to a lawyer who had nothing to do with my family and asked him to find a loop hole. I'm in love with you. I was never going to marry her. Please, believe me."

I smiled at him. "Apparently, the lawyer found a loop hole."

He wiggled his eyebrows at me. "He did indeed. All I had to do was sign over my birthright to my brother, and now, I'm free from the bonds of my fucked up family. I can't claim anything. I'll basically be non-existent."

"Are you serious?"

"I am, but here's the kicker. He was allowed to marry Paula because he didn't and couldn't inherit, since that was my birthright. So, he got a vasectomy, never telling Paula, and then married her. Now, he has to try and have it reversed, divorce Paula, and marry Kelly."

I couldn't contain my laughter. Oh my God, that is too fucked up.

Paula, I don't even feel bad for you. I suppose you aren't going to be my publisher anymore either way.

"She won't get a dime. She signed a pre-nup that states, if she cheats, she gets nothing, and my brother has a shitload of pictures of her in bed with countless men. She lost her job, her home, everything."

That was the moment it all hit me. "You walked away from everything to be with me?"

"I did. I would do it again and again."

"But you have nothing now, no family, no money, nothing."

Chuckling, he said, "Becca, I made my own money. I had my own company. They didn't take anything from me but my birthright. And I don't give a shit about that. I know how you feel about me. It's what got me through these months we've been apart."

"How can you be so sure my feelings for you run as deep as yours?"

"I was here with you for over a year. I witnessed you struggle, felt your body shake when you cried. I know how much you love him and how faithful, even in death, that you are to him. I can only dream of you giving me even half of that. I was married for seven years to a woman who was in it for the money, who didn't give a shit about me. It was all a farce. That's why I was here. I couldn't deal with the betrayal of my family and my wife. When they came up here for Christmas, it was their way of making amends. You weren't playing games with me. After what we shared that day in my bed, I knew how you felt. I knew you wouldn't have been there with me if you weren't ready. I felt you, beautiful. I felt you right here." His hand went to his heart.

I didn't say anything after that. I just sat there looking at him, looking at me.

Is he for real? Can this be for real? This is like a fantastic story I would think up and write. I was in awe of him; I am still in awe of him. As I look over at him sleeping on the couch, somehow, I don't think he is sleeping. I think he knows what I'm doing. I'm pretty sure he can hear my fingers move across this keyboard. A smile plays across my lips.

"I know you're not sleeping," I say to him.

My eyes are pinned to him as I type these words. His beautiful bluish-green eyes open, and he smiles.

"I didn't want to disturb you. You're writing again."

I laugh. "Yes, but it's not what you think it is. I'm done now."

So, ladies, or bitches who deceived me and tried to keep me from love, I want to believe you were both jealous because I got the better man. But this will continue at another time. I need to go make love to him. See ya.

Days have gone by, and I don't think I have ever been so content. I've been thinking about John, about my children. Sitting here, folded on this very desk, is the wooden picture frame that holds their photos. I still can't bring myself to open it. I don't know how to do this. It's time. Three years, it's been over three years since I last saw their faces. I'm terrified to bring them into this alternate world I've been given.

I have shared just about every aspect of our lives with him. Except for this, except for their beautiful faces, and my tablet filled with beautiful recorded chats with them. I need to do this for myself, as well as for the foundation of this relationship I'm embarking on.

Funny, I still haven't told him that I don't ever want another child. I have two of the greatest kids, and nothing will ever replace them. But I replaced John. I let another man love me, and I give my love freely to him. Shouldn't I do the same with my children? No, I can't. I just can't. I wouldn't survive it again.

He is lying on the couch watching me write here. I think he might think this is a journal or something. Maybe I'll let him read it when I'm finished. After I share everything with him, after I tell him I can't have another child. To be honest, I'm not sure he wants children himself. I should probably ask him that, but then it would just lead to the ultimate conversation of me telling him that I don't. What if he does? Will that change this? I should ask him. I am so far gone in love with him that I don't know what I would do if it was something he really wanted. Oh God, what if he leaves me because I don't want any?

Closing my eyes, I'm confident that I could survive him leaving me. But, then again, he said he was married for seven years and she never got pregnant. Was that because he didn't want children with her? Would he want one with me? I know these questions are redundant, simply because I don't have a clue what's in his head. I need to figure out a way to broach the subject. Yeah, not going to happen.

I've thought a great deal about both of you. I do feel bad for you, Paula, but you always struck me as the type of woman who would always land on your feet. I'm hoping that your husband didn't black list you, and that you are out there finding the talent. The next New York Times bestseller.

Janet, if you were in this with Paula, then I'm pretty sure you lost your job, as well. I'm not so sure I'm ready to feel sorry for you, or to feel bad in any way. You set me up. I can't help but wonder if you felt bad. Probably not. But it's all irrelevant now, isn't it? I'm here with him, with that gorgeous man you went on and on about.

He sleeps in MY bed. He touches ME the only way a lover could.

He makes love to ME, not you. It will never be you. A smile is what I wear on my face these days. He found my laugh, my warmth, and I'm not stupid enough to think it can't or won't end. With John, I took him and our life for granted. This time around, I think I learned my lesson.

We have another month of winter left, which means Christmas has come and gone again. I think we are fine with that. The plows haven't been out this way all season, so I'm pretty sure, unless they have a snow cat, that no one is coming around. We have all that time to just be together.

I should be careful sometimes. I spoke too soon. A few days after I sat down here, we had some company. Well, I didn't. We were asleep on the couch after making love in front of the fire, when someone came knocking on the door.

Half asleep, and half naked, he answered the door to see his sister.

"Can you please put some clothes on? You don't have to flaunt the fact that you're fucking her," she spat out.

He closed the door in her face. "We have company," he said with a smile on his face as he climbed back on the couch with me.

"Mmm, you're cold."

"Mmm, you're warm," he whispered, kissing me.

We got lost in each other. The way this man kisses me should be illegal. He takes his time. This time was no exception to his rule. To be honest, I forgot his sister was standing outside. I didn't care. Who would? The woman is a bitch. Not kidding. I think she might have a stick shoved up her ass. Seriously.

Anyway, in the middle of our beautiful moment of his hands touching me everywhere you can imagine, she started banging on the door. Pulling back, he looked at me, and we both started laughing.

"I suppose I should let her in?"

I shook my head. "Let her stand out there. She's a frigid bitch. I'm sure she's not even cold.

Oh my God, he busted out laughing. "I wasn't aware you knew my sister that well."

We managed to pull ourselves away from each other and put on some clothes. I went to the kitchen to make tea, and he answered the door again.

"What do you want, Alice?"

"Can I at least come in?"

"No. Now, what do you want?"

"Would you come back to your house? We need to talk. Alex is there."

"Why didn't he come down here? Oh, wait, he didn't want to get his feet wet?"

"No, I volunteered. Now, will you please come home with me."

"Well, you see, the problem with that is that I am home. I live here now."

I stood in the kitchen, smiling, as I listened to him.

"You're living with her? Richard, you are taking this tantrum a bit far, don't you think? I mean, seriously. You've been here for over a month now. I'm sure you've fucked her enough. Now, please, put your coat on and come home with me. We need to talk."

I walked into the living room as he said, "See, Alice, I haven't fucked her yet. She isn't the fucking type. But some day I hope to fuck her."

I watched as she rolled her eyes at him. "You just can't be serious, can you? This is important family business that we need to discuss."

"I'm not going anywhere. If you want to come in and discuss what is on your mind, then by all means. But I'm not going anywhere."

I couldn't help myself. I walked up to him. "You should go. I need to start dinner anyway."

"You come with." He wrapped his arm around me, pulling me to his chest.

I shook my head. "You go. I'm fine."

"I'm not leaving you again." Turning to look at his sister, he said, "Either you come in, or we're done."

"Fine." She stepped into the house.

I couldn't resist. "Would you be so kind as to take your shoes off?" Looking at Rick, I told him, "I'm going to make dinner."

I was in the kitchen, getting dinner ready, trying really hard not to listen.

"What do you want, Alice?"

"Alex's reversal might not have worked."

He laughed. "So, you're here for what? I told you I'm done with this barbaric way of thinking."

"I'm here because, well, we are willing to tear up the paperwork and give you back the title of heir apparent."

"I am going to marry Becca. I'm in love with her. I don't want that life, and I certainly don't want Kelly. That woman gives me the creeps."

Alice sat there for a long time. "Richard, I need your sperm then. We can use it to impregnate Kelly, and Alex will raise the child."

I couldn't stop myself from moving. I was in the living room looking at him. "No." It just came out. It wasn't until that moment that I realized that maybe one day I might want a child with him.

He stood up. "It'll never happen." He pulled me into his arms. Turning his head, he said to Alice, "Did you ever stop to wonder why Julia never got pregnant?"

"Because you used protection?" Alice said.

He took my head in his hands, looking me in the eyes. "I'm sterile. I can't have children. I'm sorry I didn't tell you."

My heart sank. Now that I'd figured out I might want one with him, he just confirmed he can't.

"What the fuck are you talking about?" Alice shouted.

I pulled away from him and went back in the kitchen. I felt him watch me, but he stayed. I'm not sure how I feel about this. Relief? Upset? Not really sure.

"Alice, I went a few years ago to get tested. I didn't really want a child. I knew it would be subjected to the same life we had, and no child deserves to be void of its parents' love. But I couldn't figure out why she hadn't gotten pregnant. She swore she wasn't on the pill. I can't have children. That's probably why she was sleeping with Kaleb. She wanted the hundred million."

"You're serious?"

"Yeah, the doctor's report is in the safe in my office." He was looking at me. "Alice, you need to go."

We stood there looking at each other while his sister put her shoes on and left. When the door clicked shut, he said, "I'm sorry I didn't tell you."

I smiled. "I don't want another child. I went to the doctor and got a shot. I didn't know how to tell you."

His smile started small and then got bigger and bigger. "You don't want any children?" I shook my head. "You're all right with me not being able to give you one?" I nodded. "Becca, will you marry me?"

I just stood there looking at him. "One day," was all I said, and he picked me up and carried me into the bedroom.

Let's just say that I nearly burnt dinner. He was sweet and tender. One day, I hope he will fuck me. But, until then, I will enjoy the fact that this man takes his time with me and makes me feel like I'm a queen.

CHAPTER ELEVEN

This is crazy; I mean, really fucking crazy. We were just finishing the dinner I nearly burnt.

Now, I'm smiling again. He is incredible. His mouth, his tongue, the way he loves me down there. I mean, come on! John was a fantastic lover, inventive and creative, but he didn't spend the time Rick does down there.

"I can't get enough of you," he said to me.

I mean, seriously, and the different angles, the way he moves my body. Today, he made love to me with my back against his chest.

Holy shit, ladies, if you haven't tried that, you so should.

I am finding myself insanely jealous of his wife. I so want to ask him if he was this way with her. I'm thinking not. He said she had fake boobs, and he doesn't like them, so I can't imagine he did to her what he does to me.

I breathe in deeply, just thinking about it. I swear, my panties are wet, like all the time.

Anyway, we were just finishing up when someone (you all know who it was) knocked on our door. We sat there looking at one another.

"I wish they would just leave me alone," he said softly. "I'm sorry for what is about to happen. Please, don't think I'm as crazy as they are."

"Families are crazy. I was an only child, so I don't know about this stuff. John had two brothers and three sisters, so I kind of adopted them."

We got up, and we went to put some clothes on. While he answered the door, I cleared our dishes and started to wash them. I listened in; you can bet your ass I did.

"What the hell do you people want?" he said.

"Richard, we need to talk about this." It was Alex.

Holy shit, who would have ever thought that Alexander Railing would be at my house. I had to stifle a giggle at the thought of him lowering himself to actually come here. This was going to be good. So fucking good.

"I've said all I care to say. I don't want any part of this."

"Can we at least come in and talk about it."

I heard the stomping of feet. "Do you mind taking your shoes off. We spend a great deal of time on this floor making love, and we'd like to keep it clean."

I nearly chocked on my drink. "You're not even funny, Richard," I heard Alice say.

"I wasn't trying to be funny."

"Rick, did you want something to drink?" I called from the kitchen just so they knew I was there.

I was being a bitch. But when I heard Kelly's voice, I walked into the other room.

"Why are you here? Why are you in my home?" I asked her.

"Relax, Becca, she is with me," Alex said.

"You know what, Alex? I don't work for you anymore, so fuck off. I don't want her here because her perfume makes Rick sick, and I have plans for him later." Looking at Kelly, I said shortly, "Would you please leave? Go wait in the car. I'm sure the driver could use a blow job or something." I walked over to the door, while Rick busted out laughing. "Besides, we make love on that couch every afternoon, and I certainly don't want it to smell like whore."

I opened the door, turning to look at her. She just stood there looking at me. "Get out," I said.

It was quite comical to see her face. "You're serious?"

"I am, now get out."

Alex nodded to her. She huffed over putting her high heels on and walked out the door. I slammed it shut and then walked over to lite a few candles. The place reeked. Rick just sat there with a huge smile on his face. When I went to walk back into the kitchen, he grabbed my leg.

"I'm sorry," I said to him.

"Don't be, and thank you."

He let me go, and I went back to doing the dishes.

"What do you want, Alex?"

"I want you to come back with us and go to another doctor. Richard, it's been this way for over a hundred years. You are the rightful heir."

"I signed all the paperwork and, legally, I am nothing. I don't want it. I am not giving you my firstborn child. I can't have children, and I'm pretty sure Father knew that. You love this life, but I don't. I never did. I was only in this because of Father. When I found out that the two of you arranged my marriage to Julia, I was beyond pissed off."

"Yeah, I got that when you gave up your birthright."

"I fucking seriously loved that woman. When she died, the way she died… Well, you know what happened to me. I want no part of this."

"Listen, I'm sorry about that, but you had to know somewhere that it was arranged."

"You know what? Fuck you Alex. Fuck him. How can you believe that the way we were raised was the best thing for us? Do you really think I would have allowed my child to be sent away at age five? To never know what it felt like to be hugged by his father? It's fucked up. Even if I could have children, there is no way in hell I would ever send it away, or do it with a plastic bitch who couldn't or wouldn't breast-feed them. No fucking way. Just leave me alone. Leave me out of this.

"I'm in love with Becca. I am going to marry her if she'll have me. I was happy with my life, so very happy. I was in love with my wife, and to find out she was just there for a hundred-million-dollar payout, to use her body as an incubator. She was going to leave me once she had a child."

"Did you tell her you were sterile?"

"Yes, she was my wife. Why wouldn't I have told her? Why do you think she was fucking my best friend? She wanted the money. She didn't love me."

I couldn't stand it anymore. "I love you."

He was up and across the room. He bent, wrapping his hands around my thighs, and picked me up. His mouth on mine, we moved to the wall. Then his hands were on my face, our kiss deep, different somehow.

"Say that again."

"I love you," I whispered.

We kissed again, until Alex cleared his throat. Rick put me down and turned to face his brother and sister

"You have no fucking idea how that feels, to hear someone say I love you to you and know that they mean it. For that, I feel sorry for you, for both of you. You will never know what it feels like, because the only thing people are going to love about you is your money. Alex, you are a pompous ass, and Alice, if you were anymore stuck up and full of yourself, you'd be a fucking statue in Central Park. Just get the fuck out of here and leave us alone."

"Richard, this isn't over. You are the first-born son. It's in your blood. Hell, it's your blood that will carry on our family line."

"Didn't you get the memo, Alex? I'm no longer a part of your family. I legally signed it all away. Just go, and don't come back here."

I watched as he walked to the door and opened it.

His sister sat there, giving me a hateful look. "Why couldn't you just leave well enough alone?"

"I did. He came to me."

They walked out, but Rick didn't come back into the kitchen. I walked into the living room, and he had his head against the door. Walking up to him, I put my hand on his back. "Hey."

He turned his head, and I could see the tears falling onto his cheeks. "I just want to love you, to have a long life with you."

"And we will. Come on, let me hold you." I took his hand. Locking the door, I walked him to the bedroom. "Come to bed with me."

～

I've left him sleeping in the bed. I am so pissed off at them for doing this to him. I held him while he cried. I've only ever seen Johnathan cry when our children were born. He is destroyed, and they have a tendency to not let things go.

I need to do some research.

～

Ha! I think I know how to make them leave him alone. I've emailed Alexander to come back over. I'm sure they are still at Rick's down the beach. Sure enough, he's at the door.

～

So, he came in and was nice enough to take off his shoes.

"Come and sit down. I think I have a solution to your problem. But it comes with a stipulation."

"Are you going to black mail me?"

I mean, come on, really?

"You make me laugh at how arrogant you really are. Do you really think I give a shit about you? Yeah, no. I want you to get Paula a good job as an editor. You left her high and dry, and I don't want to hear one fucking word about how she cheated on you. I was in that room, remember?"

"All right, I can do that."

"No, not can, will. I also want you to give her ten million dollars. You owe her that and more for staying married to you for ten plus years."

"Are you fucking kidding me?"

"Nope, serious. One more thing. Stay the hell away from us, from Rick."

He sat there looking at me for a long time.

"Do we have a deal?"

"If the information you are going to give me pans out, then yes, we have a deal."

I stuck my hand out. "I know you're a man of your word, so shake on it and I will tell you what I know."

He shook his head and shook my hand.

"Okay, I don't know if you read my second book. The couple in the book wanted children, but the man's sperm count was too low for them to conceive. So, I did a huge amount of research. I spoke to a few fertility doctors, which is something your high paid doctor should have suggested to you. Just because you have had a vasectomy doesn't mean you can't have children."

"I know about the reversal. I had one, but there is no guarantee, and there are no swimmers in my samples. It didn't work."

"Well, there is a way to extract them from your body. There is a difference between semen and sperm. Semen you get all the time, but the sperm is what is cut off when they do the vasectomy. It can't come out anymore, but that doesn't mean your body doesn't still produce them. They're just absorbed into your body. So, they have a procedure where they can extract it and then do IVF. You can knock Kelly up and be the head of the family."

"Are you serious?"

I laughed. "Very, it's an actual thing. I mean, people don't do it because it's very expensive. Well, for regular people it is."

"If that's the case, why couldn't Richard do it?"

"We haven't really discussed it, but it doesn't work if you're sterile. Being sterile means your body doesn't produce sperm, only semen. So, go talk to your fancy doctor and get the procedure, and just leave us alone. We want a life together, that's all. We aren't hurting anyone."

He sat there for a long time looking at me. "You really do love him, don't you?"

"After my husband died, I didn't think I was going to survive. I was up here for over a year alone. I was slowly dying. I didn't think I would ever love anyone again. Yes, I really do love him. So please, Alex, leave us alone. Let him have this life with me. He's lost so much, as well. Be a decent human being. Love your brother enough to let him go. Let him be happy."

He nodded his head. "There was a time I hated him for being born first. I hated being second. His life was so much more than mine, and I was jealous, so very jealous."

"Now, you will have the kingdom."

He shocked the hell out of me when he spoke. It was so soft I almost didn't hear him.

"Now, I'm not so sure I want it."

I smiled a small smile and said, "Well, there's always Alice."

He laughed. "I'm glad he found you."

He stood up and walked out the door. I got up and locked the door, turning off the lights. I turned around, and he was standing behind me. He didn't say a word, just picked me up and took me to the bedroom.

Let me just say that, in my whole life, no man has ever made love to me like he did.

It's been a week or so. Who the hell can tell when you are in a sex induced coma? I can't for the life of me figure out why the hell his wife would ever have cheated on him. Well, I suppose he had a job back then and probably worked his ass off. But that's not here nor there.

The weather is turning. Soon, it will be spring. We've been sitting on the porch a great deal.

"I'm going to need to go down to the house in a few weeks to clean it out and get it ready to put on the market."

"You sure you want to stay in this house? I mean, we could go somewhere else, maybe find a house together."

He laughed. "I don't want to leave here. This is where we met, where we fell in love. I want to live our life here. Is that all right?"

My heart was singing. "Of course, it is. We could sell this one and move into yours. It's bigger."

Shaking his head, he said, "No, Julia was in that house. I don't want anything that reminds me of that life."

"Then it's settled."

He took my hand in his. "Yes, it is. We still have that looming question I asked you."

I knew what he was talking about. "Rick, I'm not sure I want to get married again. Don't get me wrong, I love you. I love this life we are having."

"I understand what you are saying, but I would like to make you my wife. It's a macho guy thing."

I couldn't help it; I laughed my ass off. Climbing on his lap, I mocked, "You poor baby."

We made out on the porch for a while, then he stood up, taking me into the house. We didn't make it past the couch.

Ho hum. It doesn't get any better than that.

Weeks have passed, and spring is in full bloom. My third winter, and now I am in a pretty serious relationship. We've been in our bliss for close to four months now. Alexander and Alice haven't come back, so maybe Alex had the procedure and had his sperm extracted, and now the lovely plastic Kelly is pregnant with the next heir.

I still feel bad that Rick spent his childhood like that. I wouldn't dare allow someone to send my baby away at age five, to never hold it, hug it, or give it any kind of emotional support.

I suppose Rick is the exception to the rule that states we are the way we are raised. He is kind and caring, gentle and loving. He certainly isn't like his brother or sister.

The thought that someone would have a baby and just give it away for a hundred million dollars. I would give my life to touch mine one more time. To smell their hair when they were just out of the bath. To listen to their laughter as they play.

I'm a bit leery about his marriage proposal. I don't want to get married again, but let me just say this, ladies. He would be worth it. But what comes with his life is not something I want. Paula, you know what I mean. You've been there; although, I can recall all the times I was with you and Alex. He seemed very attentive, and it felt to me as if you two loved each other deeply.

That's something I don't understand, how you could have cheated on him. Maybe he had a small dick? Maybe he didn't push your buttons. I know people who married for money; are you one of them? It doesn't matter really. In the end, you weren't the right stock.

I chuckle to myself. The right stock. What the hell? They treat people like a breeder would. I mean, I've met Kelly, and the term airhead rings a bell. I suppose, in the end, it's the blood that matters. I am thankful I don't have the right blood.

Rick is going down to take care of his house, clean it out. Well, he burned everything, but he's getting it ready to sell. This is the time of the year that people go hunting for lake houses they never use. I want to go with him and help him, but those are his demons. He needs to put them to rest.

So, it's been a week of nothing but sex. Great sex. Phenomenal sex. He left a few hours ago to go over to his house to start clearing it out. He didn't take my Border Collie friend with him. She is laying on the floor at my feet. It's weird to have her here without him.

I'm wondering if I should worry about the fact that he's been gone for so long. Should I go over there? I'm not sure. I'll wait a bit. Yeah, no, that's not going to happen. I'm going over.

Weeks have passed me by. I still feel like a zombie. I'm still in shock. Losing someone to death is far more different than losing someone in life. I've cried for so long over him. But my heart isn't dead like it was when I lost John. I suppose, to fill my word quota, I need to tell you what happened. Not that I want to re-live this shit, but as with losing John, I found that writing it all here helped me. Well, my Border Collie friend and her fucked up human helped as well. I won't lie about that.

So, I walked my ass down the beach with Ella at my side. When we got close, she stopped and whimpered. I didn't understand what was wrong with her. I checked her paws, thinking maybe she stepped on something, but she was fine.

As I started toward his house, she grabbed my hand in her mouth, trying to pull me away. I really think she was trying to protect me. I miss her, and I feel terrible I didn't take her with me, but I had no idea where I would end up. I finally convinced her to let me go, that everything would be fine.

It wasn't fine.

It was the worst possible nightmare anyone could have. I take that back; losing John and my children in a fire was the worst.

I walked up to the house, and when I opened the French doors on the deck and stepped inside, I heard voices, laughter. I just stood there, looking around. There were toys lying around the place.

"So, you'll stay?" I heard Rick say.

"I have nowhere else to go. The question is, do you want me to stay?"

He laughed. "I wouldn't want you any other place."

That's when I heard my heart in my ears. I knew this feeling. I was going to pass out. I reached for the door frame and braced myself, but it didn't happen.

"Richard, if I stay here, I want us back."

"I'm not going anywhere. Not now, not after this. Why didn't you tell me?"

"I didn't want your father to take him. That's why I left."

His voice changed then, to the voice he used with me when he was being sexy.

"I didn't want to believe that you hated me."

I kept saying in my head, *is this real? This can't be real.* I even went so far as to pinch myself. Nope, I was not dreaming. It was Ella who made my presence known when she barked.

"Is that Ella? You still have her?" the female voice asked.

I couldn't move. I'm not so sure I wanted to move. I mean, I'm not some ugly duckling; I could stand next to a beautiful woman and feel confident. But the woman who walked out of the kitchen, well, she was a goddess. A golden beauty of unbelievable... Oh hell, the writer is stumped for a word here.

"Oh, who are you?" she said as she stopped.

My mouth went dry. Fuck if she wasn't stunning.

Then he came around the corner with a little boy on his hip. When he stopped, I saw nothing but fear in his eyes. Deep fear. I just shook my head and turned around. There was no way I was going to hash it all out in front of a baby. I walked away with my head held high. I made it to the hedge and took off running, the tears coming.

"Becca," I heard him yell.

I knew he was going to catch me, him and his long fucking gorgeous legs. I was about halfway back to my house when he wrapped his arm around my waist.

"No, let me explain," he said.

Yes, I was crying. "There is nothing to explain."

"Becca, she is my ex. That was my son."

I spun around and slapped him across the face. He let go of me and stepped back.

"Just go, leave me alone. I heard her. I heard you. I knew I shouldn't have let you in. I knew I shouldn't have loved you. I knew it was wrong."

"No, I love you. I wasn't lying about that. I want a life with you."

I laughed. "Right, sure. You keep believing that. Just go. You are a fucking liar. A fucking asshole liar."

I turned and walked away, and he didn't follow me. He just stood there. I went in the house, grabbed this stupid computer, and put a few things in a bag. When I walked out of my house on the lake, I could see him walking back to his house. His head was down, and Ella stood on the beach and watched it all happen. I can't help but wonder if she cried that day.

I waited until I could see him in his yard then got in my car and left.

So here I sit, in yet another beach house, alone. Always alone. I've told you what happened, so now I need to go mourn my loss some more. I haven't been feeling well. I think I might be sick. I've made a doctor's appointment up in the city for tomorrow, but I think I'm depressed. Who wouldn't be?

I'm at a loss, a beautiful wonderful love affair loss. I just wanted it too much, hoped for too much, needed too much. But sitting here dwelling on the life I am never going to have isn't healthy. He helped me come back from the brink of death and despair. I'm thankful for that. Thankful for him. I just wish, no, I want it all to be a bad dream. But it's not. It's reality, just like the fact that I will never see my husband or my children again.

How many times in life can your heart be broken, shattered beyond repair?

How many times does a person pick up the pieces of their life and move forward again?

How many times do we get our hearts ripped out?

How many times do we taste happiness, only to have it turn bitter on our tongues?

How many times can you fully recover from loss?

CHAPTER TWELVE

According to the doctor, I have the remnants of a slight case of the flu. Good to know. So, I took it easy for a few more days. Today, I am going to find a job. Yep, you heard me. A job. I am so sick of myself and this fucking slump I'm in. He is just a man, totally replaceable. Yeah, right, if I believed that, I wouldn't have nearly killed myself getting over the loss of John.

He isn't replaceable, and I am not even going to try. So, I'm off. Going out into the world to see what kind of trouble I can get myself into.

It's been a few days, but I got a job waiting tables at a little diner here in town. It's not that I need the money; I just need to not be alone with myself for a while. I also did something so out of character. I cut all my hair off. I'm sporting a new hairdo. I love how it sits on my shoulders. I didn't realize just how thick my hair is. It's been long forever, nearly to my waist, but not anymore.

If I must reinvent my life, I might as well reinvent myself. I've also taken my maiden name back. I don't want to be Rebecca Michaels any more, and I am certainly never going to be Becca Storm again, except for the name on this book that is never going to be published anyway.

Trust me, I know where you are, Paula, and I am going to send it to you. It doesn't matter to me anymore. I am nearing forty-seven thousand words. I may not make it to seventy-five thousand, because I'm pretty sure my story is just about over.

This journey of self-preservation has been years in the making. It took me years to come to terms with losing them, with healing the gaping hole in my heart. Don't get me wrong; the hole is still there, oozing the all-consuming goo that can at any given moment suck me back into the black abyss of darkness. But it was filled with the kindness of a man who marked my soul and gave me something I didn't think I would ever have. A second chance. But, and there is always a but in situations such as these, he too was taken away. But the hole isn't as gaping as the first. So, I'm going to move forward and heal myself this time. Hopefully, I'll be able to close the hole he made and live with the one that holds my true loves, my children.

I start my new job tomorrow, and I'm excited about it. The lovely older couple who own the place have been doing it by themselves for thirty years now. I'm not sure why she gave me the job, but she did. I'm thankful none the less, and the best part is I didn't even apply. I was sitting at the table with my applications, having a sandwich, when I looked up. Every table was full, and she was doing the best she could. But some punky kids were giving her a hard time, so I just got up and started helping. I made twenty dollars, and when it was over, I had a job. Who knew I could wait tables?

Today is my day off. I laugh. I have a day off. I worked five days in a row, breakfast, lunch, and dinner shifts. The first few days, my feet were killing me, but it fills my days and doesn't give me time to sit and sulk or think of what might have been with him.

My illness, or whatever it was, has passed and I feel alive and energetic. It's been six weeks since I left him, well, since he left me for his ex. His fucking ex, well, and his child. I really can't blame him. If John had walked back into my life, I might have done the same thing. Maybe. But then again, now that I think about it, would I?

Rick loved me in a way John didn't, couldn't. Would I have chosen John? I'm not so sure. Sorry, honey, he just loved me better. Maybe because there wasn't anything in our way. No jobs, no life, no children. But my children were my reason for existing. They were everything to me.

I had my first table with kids the other day. I thought it would be difficult, but it wasn't. It felt natural to interact with them. I can't help but reflect on how my own children would have turned out. They would both be in school. A smile crosses my face thinking about all the artwork on our fridge. I really do miss the life I had with them. I also really miss the life I was having with Rick.

How is it possible to love two men so differently? If they were both standing in front of me, I really would have the most difficult time deciding who I wanted. I know it would be John, because with John comes my children. But if my children weren't a factor, I would take Rick.

I really think I am deeply in love with that man. I don't think I am ever going to get over him. I mean, it's been two months now, and I still can feel him. I hate men.

Sorry it's been so long since I've put words to the paper. It's been about a month, and I am surviving. Actually, I'm doing fantastic. I love going to work every day. I got a kitten who is the sweetest. One of the young girls who comes in with her mother for lunch on Tuesdays wanted to put up a flyer for free kittens. Who could resist? I mean, come on, she is a giant ball of fluff, and I named her Sweetie, simply because she is so sweet. It's really nice to have someone to come home to every day.

I took her down to the beach with me yesterday, but she didn't care for it too much. I think she prefers to just lounge around all day.

She even sleeps on the pillow next to me. Yes, I'm sleeping in the bed again. I figured it's a bit ridiculous to be afraid to sleep alone. There will never be another man in my bed. If I'm being honest here, and that's what this is, honesty, no one will ever come close to him. I'm still having flash backs of him, especially when I stretch in the morning, lying in bed. I miss his mouth on me. How terrible is that?

His tongue, his lips were magic. I'm insanely jealous of the fact that his mouth has a new residence. That bitch. I know she had him first, and I suppose she has him last. But none of that matters. I love him. I will always love him.

I think I'm going to take a nice walk into town. They have a farmer's market that goes on every day. I shall be back.

Another two weeks have passed, and I think I might be in a state of shock. I mean real shock. I was at work and passed out, hitting my head on a table. The doctor came to the diner to check me out. Can you believe they still do that stuff?

He made me walk down to his office with him to get checked out. I did, but when I got there, my life changed. I am still dumbfounded, and I have no words for what the man told me.

I went back to work with a bump on my head, and now, I am sitting here hoping to God I don't throw up. I need to stay awake for, looking at the clock, six more hours. I think perhaps I need to go for a walk.

The walk went well, I have three hours left. I can't help but wonder why my life turned out the way it has. I mean, it's like you are living your dream, and then out of nowhere, a brick wall is thrown up and you crash head first into it. You recover and pick up the pieces that are left from the ashes, and you start to breathe again, start to live again, taking baby steps that eventually lead to bigger steps. Your breathing comes back, and you begin to live life again, when another brick wall jumps up in front of you and you slam right into it. You recover and take what you learned from the first brick wall and begin again.

So, here I am beginning again. Leaving, well, trying to leave him behind me, thinking I'm doing a wonderful job of living. I'm happier than I was three months ago. I know people who don't know who I am or was, because I am not Becca Storm anymore, nor am I Rebecca Michaels. It's just me, Bec Hastings. The girl I was before John, before writing, before Rick. And out of fucking nowhere, yet another fucking brick wall jumps in front of me and knocks me out.

I'm still sitting here unable to process any of this. It's not a dream because I have a bruise from pinching myself. My little ball of fluff is just sitting here watching my fingers fly across the keyboard. I think she is going to attack me.

I chuckle at myself. I feel like that dog who is concentrating, and then all of a sudden, a squirrel pops in his view and he is off chasing it. So yeah, SQUIRREL!!!

I think I'll make something to eat and then watch mindless television. Yeah, no, no television.

∿

SQUIRREL!
SQUIRREL!
SQUIRREL!
In case you are wondering, this is me in denial. I so want the distraction. I so need the distraction. I've been sitting here for literally over an hour, just looking out the window at the water.

I'm at a loss for words because I just don't know what to do, what to feel, what to say. I'm terrified. Looking around my little house filled with second hand furniture and my little garage sale finds. I suck at decorating, but at least it's mine.

Paula, I know what you're probably thinking as you read this, that I have more money than I know what to do with, but what do I need it all for? I have everything I need, and believe it or not, I make good money in tips being a waitress. More than I need really to live here. I don't have insurance, but I do have a bank account, something a great many people don't have.

I know you think I should live in some luxury house, but I don't want to. I don't need it, and isn't life about living it, not becoming a slave to it?

I'm tired now, and my hours of forcing myself to stay awake are over. I have to work in the morning.

So, good night, Paula.

Good night, Janet.

Here I am once again, walking around in a daze of sorts. To be honest, I feel like I am living in some sick and fucked up alternate universe. I suppose I should tell you what that fucked up doctor told me. I know it's truth, but I'm still in denial. I can see my body changing. Yep, you guessed it. Mr. Richard Railing is not sterile like he was led to believe. I am pregnant, nearly three months. It's probably three and a half months now, closer to four if I'm being honest.

You should probably close your mouth. I know mine has been open for some time now. I don't even know what to say really. I didn't want another child. I don't want this one. Well, that's not true. I do want it. I just don't want it with him, not after everything I learned. But I have one thing on my side. This baby is not his firstborn, so even if by some odd weird occurrence I am discovered, they can't take it away from me.

Yes, the thought to terminate crossed my mind, but it was really too late to do anything stupid like that. I just need to breathe and take it slowly. I gave my notice at work and thanked my bosses for letting me wait tables. I was thinking of getting a passport and disappearing. Then I thought about just saying fuck it and staying right here. I'm so conflicted in what I want, what to do, where to go.

SQUIRREL!!

I wish I had an alternate universe to disappear to. I keep asking myself as well as God, what the hell? But I get no answer. I never get an answer. I'm not even sure, when I die, that I am going to get an answer.

When I was prepared to go through this life alone—I mean, we are looking at, what, thirty maybe forty years left—I get this bump. A bump. Jesus.

I'm not sure I want to do this. It's a bit too late for that now, but come on. I suppose, I am just going to live this life as each moment comes, because honestly, there is no fucking planning. Plans don't work out. They burn in fires, they are taken away by ex-girlfriends, or they are changed because of a bump.

God, this is just too much. Way too much. I need to be swallowed up. Hey, I wonder if this lake has a lake monster. I've stopped looking for it, stopped waiting for it. Maybe I should just go out there and imagine it.

Am I being pathetic by saying I want him? I want a life with him? I've never needed anyone like I need him. I miss him so much it hurts, and now, I'm going to have a baby, our baby, and I am alone without him. I don't want to be. I want him. I want us.

I've been out there willing the lake monster to come, but no luck. I need to keep a positive attitude about this. No negative energy going to the bump. I want a happy bump, not a miserable one.

I bought a bike and am now peddling myself around this wonderland. I like that, in the winter, I need a jacket, not a huge winter coat. I like that it doesn't snow here, so I'm not house bound.

As I look at the word count on this document, I am just twenty-six thousand words from fulfilling my contract, which no longer even stands. I'm not sure why I am continuing to write this stupid manuscript. That's a lie. I do know; it seems to be my salvation, my piece of mind. It's keeping me sane.

I suppose I should look for things for the bump. Maybe I'll peddle into town and see what I can find. God, I can't believe I am doing this again. I didn't want to do this, especially alone.

Well, ladies, I'm out of here.

~

Days upon days have passed me by. I found a few things for the bump, but I seem to spend most of my time falling into the darkness again. I can't seem to shift gears and move beyond the fact that I am totally in love with him and I am having a baby that was conceived from that love.

I sit on the beach with my feet buried, wanting, loving a myth of a man, who couldn't have possibly loved me like I do him. If he had, he would have fought harder for me. He wouldn't have walked away so easily. He would have fought.

I guess I'm being a hypocrite here. I should have fought for him, too. But how could I have fought against a child? I don't blame him really, but then again, I do blame him. He could have had us both.

Day after day, I sit. I can't even drink tea. Caffeine isn't good for the bump. I'm not so sure I'm good for the bump.

~

As the weeks pass, the bump is getting bigger. My pants just fit me. I've managed to find a crib. Took me a week to sand it down and paint it. I chose white. I don't want to know what the bump is, so I am staying with neutral colors. Basically white. Everything is fucking white. White is the color.

Anyway, I really think I'm depressed here, ladies. I want to know if either of you have seen him. Is he miserable? Is he happy? I'm hoping he is miserable without me, that she is an evil life-sucking bitch and he regrets not coming after me. But I know that's not true. How can it be with that beautiful baby?

I'm so tired. I'm bucking for Rip Van Winkle again. Why am I like this? It pisses me off. You know what? I am pissed. I'm pissed the fucker got me pregnant and then just left me to do this alone. Not that he knew I was pregnant, but still.

I'm going to sleep.

Another month has dragged on, so I'm closing in on five and a half months, but today was a bit exciting. Interesting. So, I was sitting on the beach, of course, in tears because my life sucks and I don't know what to do with myself. So, I laid back and prayed for the lake monster to come and get me, but no such luck. I did however have the strangest feeling of being watched, but not in a creepy way. Oh, don't get me wrong, it was fucking creepy, but in a different sort of way. Like, I was being watched over. I thought that maybe, mind you I don't believe this, but maybe it was John. Maybe he was trying to hug me from beyond. I don't know. I need to get to the store. I am running low on my folic acids, and I need milk. I'll be back.

So, I'm in the market getting my groceries, not that I get a lot, but I needed to get some fruit, and some milk, and my little fluff ball needs some kitten food, and that feeling of being watched came again. I looked around but didn't see anyone.

As I was walking through the market, talking to the people I met while I was waitressing, buying some spices and fresh tomatoes, it happened again.

A man walked up to me. "Hi, how's your head doing?"

I must have given him a funny look. I'm pretty sure I did, because I had no clue who he was.

"My name is Kyle, Kyle Jones. I picked you up in the diner and sat with you until the doctor showed up. It was my table you hit your head on." He reached up to touch my head where the bump was. "That was a hell of a fall."

"It was, and thank you. I'm doing just fine."

I went to move past him. "Wait, I thought maybe we could have some coffee or something."

I smiled at him. "Thank you, but no thank you. I don't drink coffee. Again, thank you for helping me."

"No problem. I went in and they said that you quit. It wasn't that bad of a fall." He smiled. He was making a joke.

"No, I didn't quit because of the fall. I had other reasons for quitting. Now, if you'll excuse me. I need to go."

"Sure, if you want to have some tea or anything, just stop by the bank. I work there."

I nodded to him. When I turned to walk away, I walked into yet another one of those brick walls. I didn't even have to look up because I could tell it was him by his scent. How did he fucking find me? Closing my eyes, I turned away from him and started moving through the crowd of people toward Kyle, when his hand wrapped around my arm.

"No, you are not running from me again."

"Let go of me!" I yelled.

Well, when you yell like that in a crowd, people turn around, and yep, you guessed it, that guy Kyle turned around. I suppose, the look on my face was one of pure fear, because he came running up.

"Hey, let her go," he said to him.

I refused to turn around.

He laughed. "That is not going to happen."

"Please, just leave me alone." I was on the verge of tears.

"You heard the lady."

"The lady is my wife," he said.

"I am not your wife. Now, let me go." I couldn't turn around, or he would have seen my bump. I didn't want him to know. Not now, not ever. Who am I kidding here? I was so excited that he was here playing all caveman on me. But no, he hurt me.

"No, Becca." His voice was soft. "No."

Kyle bent down and looked at me. "Are you going to be all right?"

I shook my head as the tears fell from my eyes. "Please, let me go."

His hand released me, and I walked away. I didn't stop. I couldn't let him see me like this. I just wanted to go home, but he knew where I lived. I know now it was him watching me. But I came home any way. I've been on the couch crying, until now.

Now, I sit here, with my little ball of fluff watching my fingers fly across the keyboard. I wonder what she thinks.

I don't know, but I'm hungry.

After I ate, I walked down to the beach. It's chilly out, so I took the blanket and wrapped it around me. Have to keep the bump warm. I wasn't in the mood to sit, so I just walked.

Why was he here? How did he find me? I can't stay here, but he's a fucking billionaire. I'm sure he would find me no matter where I go. I am going to have to face him. I just don't want to. It hurts, and I don't want him like this. He will stay because of the bump, and I don't want him like that. It's what he did with his wife, and it's not going to be what he does here.

I turned to head back home, and he was standing on the beach. I pulled the blanket tighter around me. Closing my eyes, I headed back.

As I walked past him, I said, "What are you doing here, Rick?"

"Becca," he said in his sexy, breathy voice. The last time I heard it, he was using it on his ex.

"Don't, just don't use that voice with me. I heard what you said to her, and you used that voice. It's my fucking voice, not hers. Just go. Go back to your ex and your child, to what I am sure is now your wife."

I could feel the tears. I didn't want to cry, and I certainly didn't want him to see me do it.

"She isn't my wife. I wouldn't do that to you."

"Sure, and I suppose you walked away from your child, as well? Just leave me alone. I can't handle this. I can't handle this yo-yo of emotions you have me on. I don't want any part of this crazy."

"Will you please stop and talk to me? Let me explain?"

"I know what I heard. I know what I saw."

146

"And then you ran."

"You're fucking right, I ran. She is your ex, and she has your child."

"No!" he shouted. "No! I love you. It's always been you."

"Did you fuck her, Rick? Did you have sex with her? Did you make love to her?"

"No. No, and no. I love you. I wouldn't, couldn't do that. My heart belongs to you. I belong to you. Will you please stop running and let me fucking explain it to you."

I was walking up the steps to my deck.

"I'm not running. This is my home. This is where I live. I have friends here, people I know. I'm not fucking leaving again. You are."

I made it in the door and slammed it in his face, locking it. My little ball of fluff must have jumped five feet in the air and took off into the bedroom when I slammed the door. I felt bad for her and went to find her. Then we curled up and crashed.

Fucking asshole.

CHAPTER THIRTEEN

I don't know how long I slept, but when I woke up, I was so hungry. I ate and I ate. I felt like I was going to bust. My little ball of fluff forgave me and slept curled up in my arms. I wonder what she will make of the bump. Speaking of which, I wonder if he'll come back today. You and I both know he will.

When I opened my door to go sit on the porch with my blanket wrapped around me and my little ball of fluff in my hands, he was there. I just stood there, not knowing what to say or what to do. I didn't look him in the eyes. I couldn't, not those bluish-green pools of sex. They are trance inducing. I'm pretty sure I'm going to give in and believe his stupid mouth.

I miss him so much. I want him so much. I'm excited he is still here. I think I would have been sad if he wasn't.

"Why are you here?" I said, pushing the screen door open. Moving around him, I sat in the chair.

"Becca, I need you to hear me out. If you still want me to go after, I will."

"I saw what I saw. You were there with her. I know you kissed her."

"How do you know that?"

"Because, if it was John, I would have done the same thing."

"I did kiss her. I'm not going to lie to you. But I didn't have sex with her, not after you. I'm in love with you. Would you have had sex with John if he came back?"

I didn't say anything for a long time. "I thought about that. No, I wouldn't have. I love him in a different way, but this isn't about me. This is about you, your ex or wife, and your child."

He chuckled. I'm glad he could find humor in this. I don't think any of it's funny. I wanted to punch him.

"She isn't my wife."

"Why would you leave her? Why would you leave your child?"

I needed to know. I'm having his child, and when he figures that out, I don't want him to use it against me.

"I don't love her. I love you. When I saw your face, the pain in your eyes, it gutted me. I was in such a state of shock that I lost track of time. She presented me with a child, something I never thought I was ever going to have. You have to excuse me for that, for the shock of it all. I was coming home to you. I just lost track of time. I didn't stay there with her. I stayed at our place."

I just sat there, looking at him.

"The baby isn't mine. I had a DNA test done. She was lying. She had planned the whole thing. She wanted the money, so she thought she could just use the baby to get me to do what she wanted. When I told her what I did and that there was no chance that she would get anything, she got pissed. Becca, she was only there for less than a week. I followed her back to San Francisco, where we got the DNA test which proved it. I've spent the last two months looking for you. Why did you change your name?"

"I didn't. I took my maiden name back. It doesn't matter. None of this matters, I'm done, I'm over you." I was so lying. I wanted him to prove to me he loved me.

"You're a liar," he said softly. "I see it in your eyes."

God, I hate him. "Why would you treat me like that, like I was a second-class citizen?"

"I didn't mean to." He knelt in front of me. "God, you have to know how much I love you. I want this life with you. I want to marry you."

Shaking my head, I told him, "No, it's too late now."

"No, it's not. Why did you cut your beautiful hair off?"

I sat there staring at him. "Because I didn't want to be me, the me who loved you."

"Loved? Are you telling me you don't love me anymore?" His hand reached up to pet the ball of fluff.

I wanted to say yes, but it would have been a lie. "I'm telling you I can't do this with you. I can't have your family interfering in my life. There is more at stake here then..." I stopped.

"Then what?"

He was too close to me. I could smell him. I wanted him, needed to tell him about the bump. "You just need to leave and never come here again. I can't do this with you."

And that's when he went all lovey-dovey on me. He was already on his knee. I watched as he reached into his pocket and pulled out a ring.

"Becca Hastings, will you marry me? Let me love you for the rest of your life."

The tears came. I couldn't do this. I wanted to do this, but I couldn't. I shook my head. "No, you don't understand." I stood up, and the blanket slipped from my fingers and fell away.

"Uh," he whispered.

I turned and got one step away before he had his hand on my stomach.

"You were with someone else?" The pain in his voice gutted me.

I shook my head. "Never," I whispered, the word barely audible.

Neither one of us moved. I'm not sure we were breathing. I could feel his body shake. "Don't lie to me."

"You don't get a say in this. You left me, remember? You were with her."

"I didn't leave you. I wasn't with anyone. You own my heart. Whose baby is this, Becca?"

"It's mine. Please, Rick, you have to leave. I can't..." I went to step away, but he pulled me gently against his chest.

"Whose baby is this?" he whispered against my neck.

The tears fell. "It's mine," I whispered.

"I'm not leaving, not ever. You own my heart, beautiful. I don't care whose baby it is. I was the fool for letting you go. It's a part of you, and I will love it just like I love you. Marry me, Becca."

Swoon worthy, right? I had to let him off the hook.

"It's a part of you." I don't think I meant to say that out loud.

"Don't lie to me. I accept that I fucked this up. I can deal with the fact that you were with someone else. Was it that guy at the market?"

I didn't like his tone or the accusation. I spun around, pushing him in the chest. Turning, I opened the door and put my ball of fluff inside.

"You know what? Fuck you. If you think I'm some kind of whore, then you are truly wasting your fucking time. Go, get the hell out of here. Just leave, Rick, and don't look back. You're right. This isn't your baby, and I'm a fucking whore. Get out."

I turned to open the door, and he wrapped his arms around me. "No, Becca. No. I don't think that of you. I would never think that of you. But I understand what I did to you, and I can only imagine how betrayed you felt. It's fine. I understand."

"Let me go!" I shouted.

He let me go. "You. Are. Mine," he said in my face.

"Fuck. You," I said back to him. "I belong to no one. You are so fucked up. Just leave."

I opened my door and went in, slamming the wood door in his face. Well, that went well. Fucking bastard. How dare he think this isn't his. Bastard. I went in my room and had myself a good cry.

Now, here I sit. But not for long. I'm going to the market. I need some fresh air.

~

I just wandered around for a while. I saw that guy Kyle again. He said he worked at the bank, so shouldn't he have been at the bank? Made me wonder, so I headed over to the bank.

"Hi, I was wondering if you could tell me if Kyle is working today?" I asked one of the tellers.

"I'm sorry, but we don't have anyone that works here named Kyle. In fact, the only man who works here is Mr. Trouch. He's the bank President.

"Not even the janitor?"

I felt a bit uncomfortable. Something wasn't right. Not at all.

"No, the janitor is Mr. Simpson, the man who owns the diner in town."

"Thank you."

As I was walking out of the bank, I saw Rick standing across the street. I headed toward him.

His smile is to die for, ladies. Just saying.

"We have a huge problem," I said as I reached him.

"Yes, we do. I'm an ass and I'm sorry."

I shook my head. "Yes, you are, but it's not about that. The man at the market yesterday who told you to let me go, he told me his name was Kyle. I passed out a few weeks ago and hit my head, and he sat with me while we waited for the doctor. Yesterday, he told me he worked for the bank and asked me out for coffee. Well, today, I saw him again at the market, and I was wondering why he wasn't at the bank, so I went over there. He doesn't work for the bank. Something's not right here. How long have you been here?"

He was scanning the street. "About two weeks, maybe three."

"Where are you staying?"

"A few houses down from you. What do you think is going on?"

I stood there looking at him. He is so beautiful; he should be illegal.

"Your family. I think they are keeping tabs on you. What the hell is going on, Rick? What is your family into? Why would they follow you like that, and what is their issue with me?"

"I don't know, but come on. Let me take you home. I don't see that guy anywhere."

I didn't argue with him. I was more than a bit freaked out. It's not just me anymore; it's me and the bump. This is why I didn't want to have another child. So easily they are taken away. I need to get the hell out of here. I need for him to leave me alone and stop.

When we walked into my house, I turned to him. "You need to leave me alone. I am not about to give this baby to your fucking family. This is my baby, not yours. I'm leaving here, so please, don't try to find me again. They know now. They know."

I moved through the house, picking certain things up and putting them on the table. I ended up in my bedroom, grabbing the two bags out of my closet. I put the few things I bought for the bump in a bag, then put the clothes I can still wear in the other. Rick stood at the door, watching me.

"Becca, what would my family want with your baby?"

I just shook my head. Picking up my bags, I pushed past him back into the dining room and put the things I gathered up in the bag. I grabbed this computer and the kitten food. My little ball of fluff was curled up on the couch. I grabbed her carrier and put her in it.

"Come on, little girl. We are going on an adventure."

"Becca, what the hell are you doing?"

"Leaving. I can't stay here. You need to just let me go."

He grabbed my arms. "What are you talking about?"

I stood there looking at him. "This is my baby. Not yours. Stay away from me, from us. I don't want this. They can't have it."

"Why would they want your baby?" He actually looked confused.

I just shook my head, pulling away from him. Then I grabbed my bags and left. He followed me out. "Don't do this. I love you."

"No!" I shouted. "If you loved me, this would have never happened. You did this. Now, tell your family to leave me alone. Go home, Rick. Go back to the machine that is your life. They will never let you go."

I got in the car and drove away. I didn't know where I was going or what I was going to do, but I needed to disappear. How do you disappear? Do I know anyone who could help me disappear?

As I drove, I headed toward Napa. I had to pass through Los Angeles, so I made a stop and saw one of Johnathan's old friends. They were in the Navy together. I explained my problem to him, and he promised me he could help me. He sent me back to the vineyard and told me he would be up here in less than a week.

I always loved the drive up the coast. It was never boring. By the time I got to Napa, it was late. The main house was finished and beautiful. The lights were on, so it was nice that I didn't have to wake anyone up. The place looks great. I'm glad they went in a totally different direction to what the house originally looked like, and they didn't build it on the same spot. It's further in on the land. As I drove past the winery itself, it looked like a huge amount of progress had been made.

Pulling up in the driveway and shutting off the car meant I was safe. At least for now. Stanly won't let anything happen to me.

I grabbed what I could and made my way to the door. Stanly opened it and grabbed me, hugging me.

"My god, Bec, where the hell have you been?"

"It's a long story, a very long story. Can we stay here for a few days?"

"We?"

I held up my ball of fluff. "We."

He laughed. "You are more than welcome. Come on. I've got a guest room with your name on it. Is there more stuff in the car?"

"Yes, thank you."

He ran past me while I worked my way inside. The place is beautiful. His partner Steven came out of the kitchen.

"Oh my God, Bec," he squealed, running toward me. He grabbed me in his arms. "You gorgeous thing, where the hell have you been?"

It felt good to be wanted, to have been missed. "I'll tell you all about it in the morning. I just want to crash, and my ball of fluff needs to eat and use her box."

"Come on. I'll take her. Follow me." He took her crate and led me through the house, up a set of stairs off the kitchen. We ended up in a huge room with a large bed. "You stay as long as you want."

Stanly came into the room with the rest of my stuff. "Listen, can we talk for a minute?" I asked them.

We all piled on the bed. "What's up?"

"I think I've gotten myself in some hot water. I'm five months pregnant, and I'm not sure if this bump's life is in danger. It's a long story, but you need to hide my car, and if a man named Richard, or Rick Railing shows up, you haven't seen me. But Joe Blackshaw is coming in about a week. He is doing some checking for me on whether or not I'm safe."

"Are you kidding me?" Steven said. "Shit, it's like a spy movie or something."

"Don't worry, Bec, you are safe here," Stanly said. "You get some sleep. Stay as long as you want."

"Hell, just move in with us," Steven said. "You know you are always welcome here."

"Thank you both. For now, I would just like to sleep. Maybe take a bath."

Stanly kissed me on the forehead. "You let it all go. We will keep you safe."

Steven hugged me. "Just do what you need to do to unwind. All this stress is not good for the baby."

I smiled, the tears coming. "Thank you both so much."

Stanly wiped my tears. "Don't cry, Bec. John wouldn't want you to be sad about this. We are here for you. Relax."

I nodded. They left, and I got Sweetie's box ready for her and then fed her. I went and locked the door then dropped my clothes and crawled into the big fluffy bed and went to sleep.

It was the ball of fluff that woke me. She was playing with my hair. I was smiling when I woke. She was so cute, jumping on my head. I snuggled with her for a bit and then played with her.

My stomach growled, so I made my way downstairs to find some food. What I found was Steven in the kitchen cooking up a storm.

"Good morning, beautiful," he said. "I made all of this for you. You are way too thin to be pregnant, so sit down and let's get you fed."

I kissed him on the cheek. "Thank you."

"Stanly took your car over to the vineyard last night. It's hidden and out of the way. The staircase can be hidden as well." I watched him walk over and slide a panel out of the wall, and it popped into place, making it look just like the rest of the kitchen wall. "If anyone shows up, they will never find you. So, every time you go up there, make sure you close it. It even locks from the other side."

"You guys are too funny."

"What? You know me. I love secret panels and hiding places. Now, I made this basket up for you, and there is a fridge up there that I will stock for you. That way you can have your privacy. Just listen before you come down. We have an intercom, so when we leave, we'll let you know. But I'll be here most days."

I sat there listening to him, eating eggs, pancakes, and bacon. I was so hungry, and I need to make sure my bump gets fed.

"Do you want to talk about anything?"

"I'm not real sure that I have it in me to go over it again. Not yet anyway."

"I know. I'm sorry about everything that happened here. I can't even imagine."

"You know, it took me a very long time to come to terms with it. I'm still not sure I'm over it."

"But you're having another baby, so that's a good sign."

I laughed. "This bump was an accident, given to me by a man who was clinically sterile. Apparently, it's meant to be. I wasn't really prepared to do this again. I had made the decision to not do this. I don't think I could handle the loss if anything were to happen."

"Awe, baby, nothing is going to happen. What happened here was a freak act of nature. No one would have thought anything like this could have happened."

"I know, but you don't know the whole story, and I'm not ready to tell it all."

"You love him."

I sat there looking at him. "With everything I am. I'm just not so sure it's healthy for me. He has gutted me, and I know his family."

He came over and hugged me. "We will keep you safe. Don't worry about anything."

I felt the tears coming as I wrapped my arms around him. "Thank you."

"Come on, you finish eating and I'll go up and fill the fridge and take this basket up for you."

I nodded. "Thank you."

When I finished, I started to clean up. This kitchen is to die for, ladies. It has every little gadget you could possibly imagine. Three different kinds of coffee machines. Who drinks that much coffee?

Steven came back downstairs, told me to stop, and sent me back up here. He showed me how to lock the secret door, so I did. I think I might like being up here. I think, for the first time since this all started, I feel safe.

I am looking at my little ball of fluff all curled up on the pillow. I think she has the right idea. I'm going to take a nap.

I was woken to the sounds of voices. It was the weirdest thing. There were three distinct male voices, and as I sat up, one of them I knew instantly.

"Stanly, please, tell me if you know where she is," Rick said.

"Listen, I don't know you from a hole in the wall. I haven't seen her in over a year, not since she sold me the vineyard. What happened that would cause her to run like this?"

"I fucked up, and she won't listen to me. She's pregnant with some guy's baby, and she thinks my family wants to take the baby from her. I'm terrified that she might be... I don't know, not herself."

"Why would she think something like that? I've known Bec for years. She is one of the sanest people I know. Highly intelligent. What happened to her that would make her think that way?"

"She told me it was my baby. My family is a bit fucked up, but I removed myself from the line of succession. I'm sterile. I can't have children. Look, I am in love with her. I want to marry her."

Steven put his two cents in. "Why would you marry someone who is having a child by another man?"

"It's part of her, and I would love it just like I love her. I just need to find her."

"Why would you think she is here?" Stanly asked.

"I hired a private detective to find her, but he lost her in L.A., and, well, I figured she might have come here."

"We haven't seen her. Do you have a number or something we can call you at if she shows up?"

I heard Rick chuckle. "I do. Stanly, can I speak freely here? I'm a very rich man. I'm to the point where I can and will offer a reward of sorts for any information that will lead me to her."

"Excuse me?" Stanly snapped.

"I love her. I have to find her."

"Why? If she is running from you, then wouldn't it make sense that she doesn't want to be with you?"

"She is confused about something that happened. So much so that she slept with someone else. I just need her to understand that I didn't cheat on her. I love her."

I wanted to go down and scream at him, but he sounded different. He didn't sound like the man I spent nearly a year with. I felt uncomfortable, uneasy.

"Rick, if I hear from her, I will let her know you are looking for her," Stanly said.

Rick chuckled, but it didn't feel right. Something was different.

"She knows I'm looking for her. Thank you for your time. I hope to hear from you soon. Keep in mind, Mr. Michaels, that there will be a reward for any information leading to her whereabouts."

"Goodbye, Mr. Railing."

I was standing next to the intercom listening. I heard the door shut. Then I heard Steven.

"What the fuck? That man isn't right. There is something creepy about him."

"Yeah, you're not kidding. Bec, stay up there, and do not turn on any lights. He isn't done with us yet. I'm pretty sure he'll be back. We love you."

I slid down the wall, sitting in the near dark room. My whole body was shaking. How did he find me? I would lay money on the fact that the guy from the market was his P.I.. This is way out of line.

I just hope Joe can help me. I crawled over to the basket and got something to eat, then I grabbed this and am now sitting on the bathroom floor in the dark writing.

Paula, this is so fucked up. What kind of people are they? Why would he hunt me like this? I'm terrified, absolutely terrified. I think I'm going to bed. Fucking people.

Guess what? I can't sleep. I am that freaked out. I've been sitting here going over everything in my mind. The way we met, the things that happened. Something is very wrong. It's, and I am going out on a limb here, but it's almost as if he is obsessed with me. I don't understand why. I'm not anything special.

That man, I think he's not playing with a full deck. He moved in down the beach from me. His dog came around and befriended me. Wait a minute, she wasn't with him this last time. What happened to my Border Collie? Anyway, he found me at the lake house, then set me up to see him at his office when he knew I was back at my apartment. He followed me back to the beach house. Then that whole thing with his ex and the baby. Then he found me at my new place and moved in down the beach. He'd been there for, what did he say, three weeks? But he didn't make himself known to me until that day at the market.

Then he inferred that I am a whore, because I supposedly slept with someone else and got pregnant. Now, he's shown up here, of all places. How did he even know where the winery is? What the fuck is going on? I need to call Joe. I need to find out what the hell is happening.

I am so freaked out that I crept down the stairs to make sure the wall was secured. This just can't be happening to me.

I called Joe and told him what happened.

"Can I hire you to help me figure this out?"

He chuckled. "John would never forgive me if I didn't do everything to make you safe. I've already started my investigation. We are working on it. I've sent my brother, Al, up there to keep an eye on you. He'll come by in the morning. He already called in, and your Mr. Railing is staying in a house down the road from the vineyard."

"What the fuck? Joe, I'm scared. Can you find out about his wife? Her name was or is Julia. At least, that's what he told me. He said she died a few years ago."

"I'll be down in a few days with all that we have. Al won't let anything happen to you."

"Thank you, and hurry, please."

"Bec, it'll be fine. I can send a few more men down, make them look like workers to keep extra eyes on you."

"Really? I would appreciate that. So, Al is here now?"

"Yes, he should be on the property. I'll see you in a few days."

"Thank you."

I hung up and laid down. It was the worst night's sleep I've ever had. It's morning now, and the intercom just flipped on.

"Hi, my name is Al Blackshaw."

"Joe's brother?"

"Yes, can I come in?"

"Sure, but I'm going to need to call Joe," Stanly said.

I stood by the intercom, trying to hear Stanly on the phone. "Hold on," he said.

I think he put the phone on speaker because I could hear Joe. "Hey, brother," he said.

"Hey, is there some way you can let them know I am who I say I am?"

Joe laughed. "Stanly, he has a tattoo of Tweety Bird on the inside of his left bicep."

Al laughed. "Our sister loved Tweety."

"Okay, yes, he does. Thanks, Joe," Stanly said before disconnecting the call.

Then I heard him say, "Bec, it's safe."

I made my way down the stairs. I'll admit I was more than freaked out. The French doors leading to the backyard were right there. But as I opened the panel, I saw the doors were frosted over. I stepped into the kitchen to see one of the biggest men I've ever seen. I was stunned, actually.

I heard his breath catch when we made eye contact. We sort of just stood there looking at each other.

"Hi, I'm Al Blackshaw." His voice was gentle. Not what I expected, to be honest. He was beautiful.

I smiled. "I'm Bec Hastings."

He tilted his head. "Joe said your name was Michaels."

"It was. My husband passed away a few years ago, and I was trying to make a new life for myself so I took back my maiden name."

"Joe filled me in. I knew your husband, not as well as Joe, but we had met a few times. I'm sorry for your loss."

This man is something else, that's for sure. Absolutely stunning and saying that a brick wall couldn't do him justice would be an understatement. His arms are bigger around than my head. I couldn't stop myself from looking him up and down. Perfection is a good word. When I reached his face, I swear, I saw the man blush. He gave me a small smile and a nod of his head.

"Thank you."

"I'm here to protect you. Joe will be here in a few days."

"I'm not much to protect, but I sure am glad you're here. If I'm being honest, I'm terrified."

He smiled a soft smile, which I'm pretty sure is not his regular smile. Don't think a man this huge has a regular smile.

"You are definitely something to protect," he said softly.

Not sure that was appropriate to say, but I just smiled. I thought

Rick was beautiful and sexy. I think it was more his eyes that captivated me. This man in front of me, well, sex on a stick comes to mind. I'm sure his wife feels the same thing.

Damn, ladies, my mouth went dry just thinking about it.

"So, this is what I know so far."

He was talking again, but I was out in la la land, wondering if he was good in bed. I mean, seriously, what the hell is wrong with me? It has got to be the hormones. I remember I was a sex crazed idiot when I was pregnant with my other kids, as well. I could hear his voice, but I couldn't hear a word he was saying.

"Bec? Bec?"

I shook my head. "I'm sorry, what were you saying?"

I needed to pay attention to him.

"Mr. Railing bought a house up the street. He's there now. We've got one of our guys watching his place. We have a crew that will be here in less than an hour, that we are going to incorporate into the work crew here. The place will be surrounded. He won't get to you. I'm going to be your shadow."

I couldn't help but smile. "My body guard?" I think I'm excited by this idea.

He nodded. "Yes, I will be by your side until this is over."

"Hmm," I heard myself say, not meaning to say it out loud.

He just smiled at me and then chuckled.

"So, tell me your routine."

I laughed. "I don't have one, except to sleep and eat."

His eyes traveled down my body, landing on my bump. "How far along are you?"

"Just over five months." My hands went to my bump. "It wasn't planned. I didn't want to do this again. Not after… Well, it was an accident."

"Is Mr. Railing the father?"

I just nodded my head. "Yes, but if you ask him, I'm a whore who stepped out on him. He believes he is sterile. It's all so bizarre how it happened. I mean, the last nearly two years. I don't know what I was thinking or where my head was at, or why I even let him get close to me. But I do have to say that he sort of helped me help myself. He helped me come back from my own self destruction. I'm afraid of him now, afraid of his behavior and the things he says to me. I can never trust him. I just want to disappear and have my life with my bump, but I don't think he is going to let that happen."

He stepped forward. "I will make that happen for you. I won't let him hurt you."

I looked up. He was very close to me. "That's just it; I don't think you can stop him from finding me. He said he hired a private investigator to find me, more than once."

It wasn't what I expected when his hand reached up to touch my face. And I can guarantee you I wasn't prepared for the way my body reacted to his touch. But his fingers trailed along my jaw. "I promise, he isn't going to touch you again."

I felt my eyes close and my head tilt into his touch. "Thank you," I whispered.

It was Steven who interrupted the moment. "Oh, excuse me."

Al stepped back. "Not a problem," he said.

Steven looked at me. "You need to eat, so let's get you some breakfast. I'll go up and get your basket and restock your fridge while you eat."

I smiled at him. "Thank you."

I sat at the table doing everything I could not to look at Al. I still have feelings for Rick, as fucked up as that is. The man is incredible in bed. I know, how shallow of me to think in terms of sex right now. He is clearly a bit unstable, and I'm not so sure the sexual appetite I have at this moment in time is helping my ability to think clearly. I nearly laughed while I was sitting there, but I held it in.

Steven made me pancakes with sausage and then disappeared. Al stepped out while I ate, which I was grateful for. If it's one thing I know about myself, I wouldn't have cleaned my plate if he was standing there.

Steven came back with my basket and proceeded to fill it up again. When I finished, I wanted to take a bath, so I excused myself and headed back to my secret suite. It makes me laugh that this room is here and that I'm in it.

I stood by the window for a long time, looking out to the place where my life once was. The ground isn't scorched anymore. In fact, it is covered in grass. I hadn't realized I was crying until Al walked up behind me.

"You all right?" he asked softly. When I turned around, he was very close to me. His hand moved up and wiped my tears. "It'll be all right," he said.

I just nodded and walked away, going into the bathroom. My bath was lovely. It felt good to soak in the water. When I came out, however, Al was still standing looking out the window. When he heard me, he turned. I was wrapped in a towel.

"This is where your family perished in that fire."

It wasn't a question but a statement of fact.

"Yes."

He walked up to me and pulled me into his embrace, hugging me. I felt very small standing next to him. "I'm so sorry that this has happened to you. Joe told me about the fire when it happened. He was a mess when he came home from the funeral. Bec, there aren't words. We will keep you safe."

"Thank you." I went to pull away, but he didn't let me go. Not really.

We stood there in a strange embrace, just looking at each other. He nodded and let me go. I made my way to the closet and put on some clothes, though I'm not sure I actually wanted to put clothes on. It wasn't awkward or weird, him holding me like that. It felt natural, like I was supposed to be there.

I think I am fucked in the head. What the hell is wrong with me? I sit here perched on my bed typing these words, and he is across the room watching me. I have this incredible urge to go over and kiss him. What the fuck?

Maybe I am a mental case. Maybe Rick is right.

"You okay?" he just asked me.

"Yes, why do you ask?"

He chuckled. "Well, you're pounding on that keyboard."

I swear, my face just turned beet red. I have to go. This is so wrong.

I needed to stop and lay down. My hormones are raging, and I so want that man. A smile plays across my face as I remember how much sex John and I had when I was pregnant. I couldn't get enough of it. I don't even know Al, but I can't stop myself from wanting him.

I look around my room, thinking it's secluded here. No one would know. I shake my head; maybe I am a slut.

The door pushed open, and Al walked in with Steven trailing behind him carrying a tray.

"I made you some lunch, even though it's closer to dinner. You can't afford to skip any meals," Steven said as he set the tray down. "You eat every bite."

"Thank you, Steven, for taking such good care of me."

"Nonsense, you eat. I'll be back."

He got off the bed and said to Al, "Come on, big boy, you need to eat as well."

Al looked at me, and I laughed. "I'll be fine."

He nodded and turned to follow Steven downstairs. Me, well, I ate everything on the tray. My ball of fluff had some milk, and then we cuddled and slept some more. It just felt good to know I was safe. Even if I wasn't, the illusion was believable.

When I woke, it was dark out. I couldn't shake this feeling of being watched. It was just like at the lake. When I rolled over to stretch, I felt a pull in my stomach. I must have moaned because Al was standing next to me almost immediately.

"Hey, you all right?" he said softly.

"Yes, I think it's just growing pains."

Smiling, he went back to his chair as I sat up. I had to use the bathroom, so I climbed out of the huge, soft bed and went to do my business. When I came out, he was nowhere to be seen. As I was changing my clothes, I heard him.

"Oh, excuse me. I didn't…" he said as I turned.

I was in my yoga pants and a bra, holding my shirt in my hands. I hurried and put it on, embarrassed. "What do you have there?" I said, because frankly, I didn't know what to say. The look in his eyes was one of pure lust. I know that look. I've seen it in the mirror on many occasions.

"Some food for you." He set the tray down on the bed.

Smiling, I couldn't resist. "Well, a girl could get used to being waited on like this."

He chuckled as he left the room. I didn't mind eating alone, and my ball of fluff was ever the investigator. She needed to inspect everything on the tray while I ate. When I finished, Steven came up with my basket full of food.

"Thank you for taking care of me."

He leaned in, kissing my forehead. "Don't be silly. I'm loving it. Having people to cook for is every chef's dream, especially when one of them looks like Al."

I laughed. "He is dreamy, isn't he?" I whispered.

"Do not tell Stanly, but oh my God, is he ever. Too bad he is straight and has eyes for you." He touched my face.

"Don't be ridiculous. He does not."

"Oh, sweetheart, I know lust when I see it, and that man wants you. Go for it, I say. You're free and single."

"I wish that were true. My heart wants all of this to be a nightmare, but my body is screaming at me for sex."

We laughed for a minute, and then Al came in the room. Steven took the tray and left. "I'll be back in a little bit with your basket."

"Thank you." I smiled at him.

"How are you feeling?" Al smiled at me as he sat in the chair.

I nodded. "Tired. For some reason, I'm tired. I slept for like a year and a half, so I should be wide awake and ready to go."

He laughed, and it was such a nice laugh. In fact, it sent chills down my spine. "You weren't carrying a child inside of you."

"This is true. I'm going to do some writing. You okay with that?"

To be honest, I don't know why I asked him.

"You do whatever it is you do. I'm only here to watch over you. Our crew is here now, and everyone is in place."

"Thank you." I picked up this machine and put these words down. But, as I sit here, I can feel his eyes on me. I'm thinking I need to just go back to sleep.

~

Okay, so I'm a slut.

After I closed my laptop, I pushed it aside and laid down. You would think I would or should have looked away from him, but I didn't. I laid there looking at him.

He has a short haircut, a chiseled jaw, and a few scars on his chin, from fights I'm sure. He is wearing a t-shirt that should be illegal on him. Not even flexed, his muscles are very noticeable. He just looks like a sculpture of stone.

Our eyes met, and I watched his soften. I swear to you that they were calling me. I hate raging hormones. My body came alive, and I sat up.

Hold on to your seats, ladies, because I might get detailed here.

I couldn't stop myself. I got up and walked over to him. He didn't move as I stepped between his legs.

"Who are you?" I whispered.

He didn't answer me, and he didn't move. I swear to you, I have to be on some kind of robot mode. My leg moved on its own around his, and I found myself sitting on his thighs.

When his hands came to rest on my hips, I wanted nothing more than to fuck him. I swear, I am not this woman. Something is drawing me to him. He is here to do a job, and I am coming on to him. And, trust me, I am so coming onto him.

"I don't know what's wrong with me," I whispered as my fingers touched his face. "I can't seem to stop myself. I'm really not usually this forward."

His eyes closed as I touched him. "I'm not complaining. I've been sitting here fighting with myself."

He shifted his body so he was sitting up straight and our faces were even.

"Fighting yourself over what?" Trust me, I have no idea where the hell this voice was coming from.

"Over climbing in that bed with you. I've never had a reaction to a job like I am having with you."

"Is that what I am? A job?" My fingers touched his lips. I felt so God damn sexy.

"You are, but I think it's about to become something more."

His eyes still closed, I felt him moan.

"Why is that?"

His eyes opened, and he moved forward, his hands grabbing my face, and his lips searing mine. I swear to God, I turned to jelly in his arms. This huge muscle-bound man was so gentle, so tender, so fucking good, it was ridiculous. The kiss went on forever. He stood up and walked us to the bed, laying me back, his leg between mine.

When he pulled out of the kiss, I was breathless. "This should not happen."

"What's that?" I asked him.

His knee pressed into me, and my back arched. I swear, I had an orgasm. His hand cupped my breast. "This," he groaned as he kissed me again.

I let him touch me, and trust me, he touched me for quite some time. Don't think for one minute I didn't touch him back. It's not true what they say about men built like him, that they are muscle-bound because they have small dicks. Wrong. This man's cock was fucking huge, so huge that I want it buried deep inside of me. I wanted to see it, to touch it without jeans. I wanted to wrap my mouth around it. But he stopped us.

"Bec, I want you. I want to fuck you this side of Tuesday, and I want to make love to you. But I am on a job here. I have never crossed this line. Please, understand that. I just can't help myself. I don't know what it is about you."

"I understand. I do. I'm sorry. I didn't mean for this to happen."

He chuckled. "I'm not sorry. And just for the record, I wanted to make the move. I want this to happen, but I'm on a job here. I can't lose my focus. I'm not saying this isn't going to happen again, because I'm pretty sure it's going to, but I would like it to be under different circumstances."

His words were kind and tender. His eyes told me he was telling the truth. His lips, well, they were trying not to.

We finished our kissing and touching, and he got up. I watched him adjust his huge cock in his jeans. I swear, I was waiting for the head to pop out of the top. Me, I just rolled over and went to sleep. Well, tried to sleep. My panties were soaked, and I was throbbing. I wanted him. God help me, my heart is still wanting Rick, but my body wants Al.

I woke to voices; the intercom was on. It was Steven and Stanly talking. It was dark in my room. I got up and moved to the intercom.

"She needs to eat. Bec, we have dinner for you and Al. If you want to, you can come down, or open the door and I'll bring it up. Oh, hey, Al," Steven said.

"I'll take it up. She's still sleeping."

I heard the tray clinking. "Thanks, just leave it up there until morning," Stanly said.

Then the intercom went off. I went to the bathroom. When I came out, the tray was on the bed and Al was sitting there waiting for me. I smiled and climbed on. We ate in the near darkness, not saying a word.

When we finished, I watched him put the tray on the floor. "I think we should talk."

I smiled at him. I suppose, this is where he gently lets me down.

"It's fine. I get that I am the job. I also get that we really know nothing about one another. Not to mention I am nearly six months pregnant with another man's child." I laughed. "It's hormones. I am so damn horny it's not even funny." When I looked at him, he looked a bit upset. "No, no. Oh, God, it's not what I meant. I'll just shut up."

He smiled at me, his hand reaching up to move my hair off my face. "I wasn't going to say that. It doesn't matter to me that you are pregnant with another man's child. That wouldn't have stopped me. What I wanted to say is, when this is over, I would very much like to take you to dinner."

I smiled. "Yeah?"

"It's been a very long time since I've been attracted to someone, and I have never been attracted to any of my jobs. But the minute I saw you, something in here," he touched his chest, "felt different. I feel this immense attraction to you."

I had to giggle. "I know, right. I don't know what it is, but fuck, I just want... Well, earlier, it was obvious what I wanted."

He reached around me, pulling me onto his lap. "What do you want?" His breath was hot on my lips, but he didn't kiss me.

"I want... I... um..."

I couldn't form a fucking sentence, so I didn't say anything. We just sat there, less than an inch apart, looking at each other.

"Tell me, Bec. Tell me what you want."

My eyes closed, and I swallowed. His hands moved down to my ass, and he picked me up so I was straddling him, pulling my core to his very hard, deliciously huge cock. I swear to God, I came right there. He knew it because he smiled a small smile.

"Tell me, Bec." His tongue came out and trailed along my lip.

"I want..."

I swear to you, I had nothing in my head. I just wanted to fuck this man and to have him fuck me. There was no rhyme or reasoning to it. He was beautiful, and I knew he would protect me with his life. I've known him for two days, and I want him.

It was like this with Johnathan, as well. It was an instant connection. But, with this man, it's more than the connection I had with Johnathan. This is much more than what I felt with Rick.

I moved away from him. At first, he felt a bit reluctant to let me go, but he did. I got off the bed and went into the bathroom. I didn't know what to do. I wanted him. God help me, I wanted him.

It took more than a few breaths to get my composure back, but I did. Opening the door, I went to walk out but he was standing there. No words were said; they weren't needed. For some strange cosmic reason, we were connected. I thought I knew what attraction was, what physical attraction was, but this man, this feeling, was nothing I had ever felt or known.

He was gentle in his assault on my body, and I will say assault. It was intense. He picked me up and walked over to the bed. First, my shirt came off, then his. I mean, come on. Talk about sculpted Norse Gods. Fuck if he isn't perfection. He has a beautiful tattoo across his chest. My hands just moved on their own across his pecs, down his stomach, touching his perfectly defined abs.

Holy shit, I felt my panties soak through. What the hell is wrong with me?

My fingers slipped into his jeans, and I undid the first button, then the second, then the third, I love button fly jeans. He stood stock still as I undid his jeans. When I finished, I moved back to look at him. he didn't have anything on under his jeans. I licked my lips, and he was on me.

"Never has a woman looked at me like that," he groaned as he lifted me onto the bed.

My hands found their way to the prize, and holy fucking shit. He was huge, hard, and dripping. I pressed on his chest, and he rolled off me, laying on his back. To find the words to describe what he looked like, I'm not sure I could.

Perfection. There's a word.

Fucking spectacular.

Glorious.

Incredible.

My hands tugged his jeans off, and they landed on the floor when I tossed them over my shoulder. My eyes never left his body. I couldn't help myself.

Beautiful.

Huge.

I watched as his hand reached for his cock. He pumped it a few times. My tongue licking my lips, I shook my head and he let go. I wanted him. I wanted him in my mouth, and I'm not going to lie about that fact.

My hand reached for him. My fingers didn't fit around him, but I wanted him in my mouth, down my throat. Slowly, I leaned in, his hand wrapping around my head, grabbing my hair.

"Bec," he moaned.

"Don't," I whispered.

He let go of me. My mouth opened, and my God, it was so easy to wrap my mouth around him. I was so driven to have him this way. I didn't even know this man, but for some weird, strange reason, I felt like I did. The connection that pulsed through me was one of… for lack of a better word, destiny.

Yes, this man was my destiny. Slowly, I sucked, licked, and fucked him with my mouth, gradually working him down my throat. His moans and ahhs drove me. I wanted him. Once he was completely in and my nose touched his stomach, I swallowed, and I felt his warmth jet down my throat. With each pulse, I swallowed slowly, pulling him out. When my lips wrapped around his perfect head, I just let my mouth massage the last of him out.

Fuck if that wasn't the most erotic blow job I've ever experienced. When I finished him off, I sat back and looked at him. He was jelly, and I couldn't hide my smile. Slowly, he opened his eyes and turned his head to look at me.

I smiled. "I'm not sorry," I whispered.

He chuckled, his hand wrapping around my arm and pulling me down next to him.

"I have never…"

"I'm not sorry."

He shook his head. "I'm going to be honest here."

I couldn't help but smile. He was going to say something to

cushion the blow of him telling me it can be nothing more than this. I'm all right with it.

"Al, let's just let this be what it is. My life is complicated," I rubbed my belly, "and it isn't going to get any less complicated. We are both here now, and obviously, we are both attracted to each other. So, it's all right. You don't need to make excuses or feel guilty. I wanted to do it, and I'm pretty sure I'm going to want to do that at least one more time."

He sat up. Laying me down, he snuggled into my side. "Shut up for five minutes."

I giggled.

"What I was going to say is, I've been with many women but never without protection. I have yearly physicals and a clean bill of health. I don't have a steady relationship, and I haven't had one in a very long time."

"Why?"

"Because I had my heart ripped out and handed to me. It was a long time ago, but I am the job. Sometimes, it takes me away for weeks at a time, and women don't like that. It's just easier and less complicated. I really don't like conflict with women. My job is to protect them, and well, I really enjoy the female body."

I laughed. "Well, mine isn't much to enjoy right now."

"That's where you are wrong. You are fucking beautiful. My point here is, I would really like to see you outside of the job, to take you to dinner, maybe hang out. I have never felt this attracted to a woman in my life, even with the one that ripped my heart out. But with you, it's like I am connected to you. And, just for the record, I have never had a woman swallow my cock like you just did."

I couldn't help it; the giggling took control. When he flicked my bra clasp open, and his mouth wrapped around my nipple, I stopped laughing.

∽

I sit here writing on this stupid machine. My life is so fucked up, and in case you are wondering, no, we didn't have sex. He feasted on my nipples, and then we honestly fell asleep wrapped around each other.

I am such a slut. Maybe Rick was right in assuming I'm a whore. No, fuck that.

Al is in the shower, and the sun is just cracking the sky. I'm worried about what Rick is up to. I wish Joe would get here. I need to know what the hell is going on.

You know, I've been lying in this bed for a few hours trying to sleep. I can't understand how my life got so fucked up. I mean, even before Johnathan, I was in and out of relationships. Looking for love, looking for acceptance, looking. Always looking. For what, I'm not sure. After they left me, I was positive that I wanted to be dead. I wanted to be with them.

Then I met Rick, and he helped me. Maybe he even saved me from myself. But did he? What happened to him that he has become so scary and obsessed with me? Was he always this way?

I should call you, Paula, and ask you what you know, but I'm sure you had to sign a non-disclosure agreement.

I suppose, I was living in my own little bubble of life and didn't really pay any attention to what was going on in the outside world.

As I'm sitting here, the bathroom door has opened and the Norse God just walked out, buck ass fucking naked. Holy fucking shit, ladies. My God, my panties are soaked. What the fuck?

He smiles at me as my fingers move across the keys.

"Whatcha doing?" he asks.

I just smile at him. "Fulfilling a quota."

"How do you type without looking at the keys? Better yet, how can you type and talk at the same time?"

"It's easy. I wrote my second and third books with babies running around. It's just something I can do."

Okay, I need to go. His beautiful cock is getting hard.

∼

Well, that just sucked, and I don't mean that in a literal sense. Steven interrupted me as I was getting off the bed.

"Bec, there are three cars coming up the drive."

I looked at Al, who was getting dressed, and rather quickly.

"I'll be back. Follow me down and lock the wall. Do not come out. Is that understood?"

Bossy much, but I nodded. The fear that overtook my body was very real. I didn't want him to go, but Rick could easily overtake Steven or Stanly.

"Please, come back," I whispered to him as he unlocked the wall.

I watched him leave, and then I locked the door and flew up the stairs to stand by the intercom.

"It's not my brother," Al said. "Is there someplace you can hide if needed?"

"Yes, we have a safe room," Stanly said.

Al looked at him. "Bec, get your ass down here now."

I grabbed my computer and my ball of fluff and ran down the stairs. When I got to the front door, Steven grabbed my arm and I followed him into their office. I watched as he opened the safe room. "Get inside," he whispered.

He followed me and turned on a bank of televisions and flipped some switches. "You can see and hear everything. Do not come out."

He ran out and shut the door. I heard the steel bars move into place. Fuck. I am sitting here watching the cameras.

Oh my God. Oh my God. Shit hit the fan. Big time.

It was Rick, and he had a few guys with him. One of them was that Kyle guy from the market, which turned out to be his P.I.. This is how it went down.

Al sat on the couch, and Stanly answered the door.

"Mr. Railing, I told you before that she isn't here. It's not even six in the morning. Why are you here?"

"This is Kyle Jennings, a private investigator. I hired him to find her. When she ran this time, he tracked her here."

"Mr. Railing, this is becoming tedious. Do I have to call the police?"

I sat there watching Steven close the secret door then walk into the front hall like he just got up. "Honey, what's going on?"

I had to smile.

Stanly looked at him. "Mr. Railing thinks Bec is here."

"I brought some police with me, with a search warrant. I don't believe you."

I watched Al get up and walk to the door. "What are you talking about? On what grounds?"

Rick stood there, dumbfounded. "Who are you?"

"I'm Alexander Huntington the third. Who are you and why are you looking for Bec?" He played the part, turning to Stanly. "I thought you said she wasn't here."

"She's not. What reasoning do you have for a search warrant?"

Rick just stood there. He didn't know what to say. Looking at Al, he said, "Why are you looking for Bec?"

"She is carrying my baby, if it's any business of yours. She agreed to marry me, and then she took off. Are you the reason she left?"

I sat there watching Rick look at Kyle, then back to Al.

Stanly asked Rick, "How do you know about this place?"

Al just looked at Rick. "Can I see your search warrant? I work for the F.B.I., and I'd like to know what this search warrant is for."

Rick just looked at him.

"You don't have a search warrant, do you? Why are you looking for Bec?" Al was being persistent.

"I love her. She loves me. We had a disagreement, and she left me."

Shaking his head, Al said, "I'm sorry, Mr...."

"Railing."

"Mr. Railing, but Bec and I are getting married."

"No, she is going to marry me."

"Mr. Railing, the ring she wears on her finger is mine."

"No!" Rick yelled. "No! She loves me."

Steven walked back into the room. "I've called the police. Please, leave. Bec is not here."

Rick stood there looking at Al like he wanted to kill him.

"Listen, if it will make you feel any better, and if you will leave us alone, come in. Come in and look around. Check the closets, look under the beds. Do whatever you need to do to just leave us alone. She isn't here, she hasn't been here, and I don't know why you would think she would return here. This is where her family perished. Mr. Railing, please, just leave us alone." Stanly turned to Al. "I don't know what to tell either of you, but she just isn't here."

Rick stood there for a long time, looking at him. I could see the lights from the squad cars flashing on the door.

By the time it was over, Rick had left, and Al went back to the couch. I waited for Steven to come and get me. It was already mid-morning by the time he did. Al was waiting for me.

"Joe is on his way. Come on, let's get you dressed and fed. This is going to be a long day."

I hugged Steven and Stanly. "Thank you. Joe is supposed to be bringing me a new identity, and I will get out of here."

Stanly smiled at me. "No, Bec, we want you to stay."

I was too tired to argue. I came up to my secret room and crashed.

When I woke up, it was because I felt like I was being watched. Opening my eyes, I realized it was getting light out, and there he was. I watched as he got up and walked over to the bed, his clothes falling from his body as he moved. By the time he reached me, he was naked and hard. My mouth watered. I never really enjoyed giving blow jobs. I did it, but you all know it's a take or leave kind of thing. But this man, this cock, I want.

He climbed into the bed, pulling me into his arms. We didn't talk as he slowly removed my clothes, his hands touching every part of my body. We kissed for a few minutes, then he rolled me on my side, so my back was facing him.

I nearly burst into tears when his hand covered my stomach and he held my bump, kissing my neck. I don't remember him moving his hand to my thigh, picking it up as he slid his leg between mine.

Then I felt his fingers on me, touching me gently, pinching my bud between his fingers. I swear, my body just let go, and an orgasm shook me to my core. Holy shit, it was intense.

"That's it," he moaned. "I want you wet."

God, I was helpless as he continued to touch me, arousing me again. My body tensed and tightened as he built me up again.

"I feel you, Bec. Let it go." The heat from his breath on my neck was making me crazy.

Then his hand was gone, and I felt his cock there. Oh God, he was going to fuck me. I thought I'd died and gone to heaven. So slowly, he worked that giant piece of soft steel into me from behind.

"Oh God," I whimpered as he filled me.

"So tight," he moaned as he based himself.

He didn't move at first, waiting for me to adjust to his size. His fingers found my bud again, and it was only a matter of seconds and a few slow movements of him inside of me and I lost it again. He made love to me for such a long time. Slowly, methodically, so much tenderness, so much...

His hands were everywhere, squeezing my breasts, pinching my nipples. He bit my neck, kissed me. I don't think a man has ever taken this much time making love to me, and that's what he was doing. He was slowly making love to me.

"One more, beautiful. Give me one more." His hand moved down my body, over my bump, where he paused to hold it, then down to my core. He brushed his fingertips along where we were joined, and my body shattered. I shattered. He shattered.

Never have I ever felt like this. Never.

His kiss was different, deeper, sensual. He slipped out of me, rolling me over into his arms, and held me. His hand on my face, wiping my tears as they gently fell from my eyes. His lips loved mine, and yes, ladies, I felt loved, like I have never felt before.

"Incredible," he whispered. "Fucking incredible."

He tucked me into his chest, cocooning me, and we fell asleep.

CHAPTER FOURTEEN

I woke to feel his fingers trailing down my side. I think he knew I was awake.

"I'm not sorry for what I did," he whispered.

No one in their right mind would ever think this badass man could or would be so gentle, so tender, so loving, and yes, ladies, he was loving. His voice is so soft you wouldn't believe it came out of this glorious body I was cocooned in.

The smile just came. "I'm glad you're not sorry."

"I have never had unprotected sex. I hope you know you can trust my health."

I couldn't help it; I giggled. "We shared something very powerful, and you want to start this conversation with that?"

He chuckled. "Yeah, I suppose that wasn't very romantic."

I was still giggling. I think I was high or something. "Nope, not one bit romantic. But as long as we are on this road, can I ask why you did that?"

"With you, it's different. With you, I don't want this to be over. Weird, huh?"

"No, not that, why did you make love to me?"

He laughed, pulling back so he could look at my face. "Because I couldn't stop myself. I wanted you." He kissed me. "Bec, please, don't think I'm using you." He was so sweet, so tender with his touches and his words.

I had to pull away. I couldn't do this. I couldn't allow myself to have an emotional connection with him. Not with this mess, with Rick, and the fact that, today, I am getting a new identity so I can disappear. I just can't do this. I got out of bed and headed to the shower. As I was drying off, I heard Steven on the intercom.

"Bec, I made some lunch. Joe called and said he should be here in about twenty minutes. It's safe to come out."

I got dressed while Al sat in the chair and watched me. I wasn't sure what I saw in his eyes; I'm not sure I can care. I mean, seriously, I am some kind of fucked up. Fucking hormones. I wouldn't have done that if I wasn't pregnant. I know me. I was having a hard time looking at him. So, I just went downstairs.

Steven kissed me on the cheek when I walked into the kitchen. We sat in complete silence while we ate, Steven watching me like a hawk.

"You all right, Bec?"

"Yeah, I'm just tired of this shit. You know I didn't ask for this. Everything I lost, everything I've done to survive them, and now, here I am, having another baby, obviously alone, and I have a fucking crazy man stalking me, hunting me. I guess I can feel myself sliding backwards again. Joe is bringing me a new identity, so hopefully, I can disappear somewhere and just be alone with my bump and my ball of fluff."

Al sat there staring at me, his eyes never wavering. I know he wanted to say something, but he didn't have any right to say anything. I don't even know him. I mean, yeah, we had sex, but isn't that all it was? I'm so fucking conflicted.

"I think I should be punished for bad behavior or something," I mumbled.

When I finished, I got up and went to walk out the door.

"No, Bec, you can't go out there," Steven said softly.

"I need some fresh air. I need to think, and I can't do it sitting in the house."

The back of the house opens onto the bulk of the estate, but it's not visible from anywhere really. When I opened the door, I saw a chair and went to sit in it. Al came out and sat next to me.

"Do you want to talk about what happened?"

"I don't know what the hell happened. I can't pretend that was anything other than what it was. I am so fucked up right now. I just need to get out of this mess. I need him to stop this shit so I can just go live by a lake and be me. Well, the me I've become since they left me."

I watched as he pulled his phone out of his pocket.

"Joe is here." He smiled and then chuckled. "They're all sporting their F.B.I. jackets. This ought to be fun. Come on, let's go see what my brother has to say."

"You go, I'm going to sit here for a while."

"Bec, I'm not leaving you out here alone. My job is to protect you."

I looked at him, like really? I mean, four hours ago, he was buried balls deep inside of me. But he needs to protect me.

"Fucking hypocrite," I muttered as I got up.

He grabbed my arm and turned me around. "No, Bec, I'm not."

I looked at his hand wrapped around my arm. "Yes, Al, I'm afraid you are. Please, let me go."

His hand released me, and I walked into the house. I ended up in the living room, sitting in a chair. I heard the cars pull up, three in all. A few minutes later, Joe walked in. He saw me sitting in the living room and made his way to me.

"Let me get Stanly over here," Steven said.

"How are you doing?" Joe said to me.

I just sat there looking at him. He was one of Johnathan's best friends. Before I knew what was happening, the tears came, and I was in his arms, sitting on his lap, cradled in his embrace. "I got you, Bec," he whispered against my neck.

It was weird how the sobbing just started. I don't think I've cried like this since it happened. I couldn't stop. I know I screamed a few times, but he didn't let me go. I felt us move, and he sat us down on the floor. But he held me. Stanly came in, and he and Steven stood there crying with me.

Eventually, I calmed down, but Joe didn't let me go.

"I just miss them so much, Joe. I've fucked everything up," I whispered.

"I know, beautiful. I miss him, too. And you didn't fuck anything up. It's called life. We all make mistakes. Come on, let's get you cleaned up. I've got some information that you might find interesting." He let me go a bit, pulling back to look at me. His hand came up and wiped my tears. "You're going to be just fine. He didn't love you because you were weak. You're a strong woman, Bec. You'll get through this."

I just nodded and got up. Steven ran over and grabbed me in a hug. "God, beautiful. Come on." He led me to the half-bath off the hallway.

When I came out of the bathroom, Al was leaning against the wall. He didn't look happy, but you know what? I don't care. Joe has my new identity, and I am leaving. I just stood there looking at him. I went to walk away, and he stepped in front of me.

"We need to talk," he said softly.

I just nodded and moved around him.

Joe filled me, well us, in on my friend Rick.

"This is big, huge actually. I'll warn you now that it's really bad news, upsetting beyond what I expected. Apparently, Mr. Railing is a very troubled individual. He has been in and out of psychiatric hospitals for the last fifteen years. His wife disappeared a few years ago, and no one has seen her. The authorities believe he killed her, but they've never found enough evidence to officially link him to her death." Joe looked through a file he had, handing me a picture.

I took the picture, and my breath hitched in my chest. "She looks like me."

Al reached for the picture, looking at it then at me. I could see the anger in his eyes.

"She's been missing for two years. From what I've learned, she couldn't get pregnant, and the condition of their marriage was that she had to produce an heir. All three of the Railing children were sent away at age five to a conditioning school. The doctors think he cracked in his mind, separated, and has a spilt personality from the conditions of the school they were sent to. I've had one of my guys checking the school out. Seems it's for the elite rich. Costs a million a year per kid to go there.

"Bec, he might think in his mind that you are his wife. We found documentation that he had a vasectomy ten years ago. He didn't want his children to go to this school, so he fixed it so he couldn't have children."

"But this is his child. How is that possible? This woman showed up at his house and said she had his child. That's when I left."

"It happens sometimes. Do you know what her name was?"

I shook my head as I watched him look through his file. Pulling out a picture, he handed it to me. It was of Rick and the woman.

"Her name is Naomi Trace. Her body was found a few months ago in a river just outside of Seattle."

I felt myself get sick. I was up and moving to the bathroom, where I tossed my lunch. Oh my God, he killed her. What the fuck? I was so freaking out. I made my way back to the living room.

"What about the baby she had?"

"There was nothing about a baby."

"Joe, she had a baby with her. Do you think he killed the baby, too?"

"I don't know," he said with a sick look on his face. He pulled his phone out of his pocket. I sat and watched him pull a laptop out of his bag. "Stanly, do you have Wi-Fi out here?"

"Yes, let me get the password for you."

I sat there watching Joe's face as he logged into the Wi-Fi and went to work. "Son of a bitch!" he yelled, making all of us jump. Al was standing behind him. His eyes shot up to me.

"What?" I said.

Joe turned the computer screen around to show me the image he'd come across. It was from one of my first readings in San Francisco. In the background was Rick. "Oh my God," I whispered. My eyes looked at Joe.

"He knew who you were. When was this picture taken?"

"I was just pregnant with…" I hadn't said her name since that day.

"Anna?"

I nodded as the tears fell. "Yes."

Joe got up and walked out of the room. He went out the front door. I could hear him talking, then yelling. Al just stood there looking at me. I could feel his eyes on me. I got up and went upstairs, locking the wall panel behind me.

I know what Joe was doing. I could feel it. Rick murdered my family. I can't do this. I can't handle this. He murdered them; I could feel it. He would go after Al now. I spun around and made my way back downstairs.

Joe was in the kitchen. "He killed them, didn't he? He started the fucking fire, and he killed them. There wasn't an investigation because of the wild fires. That's what you are going to tell me, right? He killed his wife, and now he's coming for me." I turned to see Al. "You staked your claim on me. He is coming for you. I can't do this, Joe. I can't. He needs to be stopped."

Al walked up to me, putting a gun in my hand. "Don't go anywhere without it. If you feel threatened at all by him, flip the safety off and pull the trigger."

I just looked at him, shaking my head. "No, no. I can't. I won't."

Joe walked up to me, pulling me into his embrace. "Bec, I am not going to let anything happen to you."

I could see the pain in Al's eyes. He turned and walked out of the room. I heard the front door slam as he walked out.

Now, I sit here, in my secret room, terrified. This is all so fucking bizarre. He has to be stopped. There are fifty men on this property, waiting for him. Waiting for him to come for me. I'm tired of running, tired of this fucking game.

Paula, I am personally holding you and Janet responsible for not telling me this shit, for not letting me know he was a fucking crazy person. If he kills me, this is on you.

∾

I nearly threw this fucking machine across the room. I laid in the darkness and sobbed. I mean, what the fuck is wrong with me?

My bedroom door opened, but I knew it was Al. He is pissed off, and I think I know why.

I just laid there waiting for him to come over to me, but he didn't. He sat in the chair. I could hear his breathing; it was deep so I could tell he was still pissed off. I didn't care. I really didn't. I'm hormonal, and yeah, if I'm admitting shit, I would probably let Joe fuck me. I just don't want to feel anything. I know that's a fucking cop out, but too fucking bad. I am so pissed off that this fucker could have killed my family. My children. And now, now, he is fixated on me. Well, that's not true either. He has been fixated on me for years.

I want to talk to fucking Alexander, the bastard, or their bitch of a sister, Alice. Why wouldn't they warn me? Why would they let this go? No wonder his sister was taken back by me. I look just like her.

I couldn't stand listening to him breathe anymore, so I sat up. "What?" I snapped at him. "What is your fucking problem? Let's just add even more shit onto this fucking pile of bullshit that I am sitting on. Come on, Al, let me have it."

He didn't say a word, but his breathing increased. Jesus, he sounded like a fucking pissed off bull. Not that I know what a pissed off bull sounds like, but I can imagine. I can't help but think of a cartoon bull. I almost giggled.

"I didn't like what I saw. For the first time in my life..." He just stopped talking.

"Just go. Please, just leave me alone."

"I'm here to protect you. I'm not going anywhere."

I'm such a bitch. "You sure you're not here to fuck me?"

He was off the chair, pulling me off the bed by my arms. He freaked me out, he moved so fast. I mean, this is a big room, and he was nearly on the other side of it. "Is that what you think I did? Fucked you?"

I laughed. "Isn't it? I'm just the job, Al, nothing more."

"You're wrong."

"Am I? Am I really? When this is over, you'll go your way and I'll go mine. I'll go off and have my demon spawn child, and you will go back to fucking random chicks. Just let me go." I tried to get away from him.

"No, Bec. No."

He pulled me right up to his face. I could feel the hot puffs of his breath on my lips. I thought he was going to kiss me. I tilted my head up. "You want to fuck me now, don't you?"

Trust me, I have no clue what the hell is wrong with me. I just spent hours crying like a baby. Now, here I stand, challenging a man who I know could literally split me in half, taunting him into fucking me. I'm nuts.

"Trust me, sweetheart, if I had fucked you last night, you wouldn't be able sit that perfect ass down today."

I laughed right in his face.

"I didn't like the way my brother was holding you. You should have been in my arms."

"Why? Because you think you have some claim on me? I've known Joe for nearly fifteen years. He was one of my husband's best friends. Why wouldn't I break down in his arms? Why wouldn't I let someone who has a clue how I feel hold me while I lost it? You need to get a grip. You don't own me, Al. You fucked me, and I gave you a blow job. You don't know a fucking thing about me."

He laughed. "I know you're scared. I know you want me right now as much as I want you. I know that, when this is over, I'm going to take you out. I know that I am going to be the last man you make love to."

I laughed. "I wouldn't bank on that."

"You make me fucking crazy," he said as his mouth covered mine. His hands let me go and wrapped around my head as his lips seared mine.

Fuck, this man is potent. And before you even ask yourself, yes, we had sex. No, he didn't fuck me per se`, but he did slam that magnificent cock into me a few times. God, it felt so good. He is huge, and if I'm admitting things here, I could fuck this man three maybe four times a day. The way he flicks his hips… Shit.

We fell asleep with him holding me.

~

I woke up this morning to hearing voices again. I was alone in bed, which didn't surprise me. I felt bad that I'd treated him so badly. But, what can I say? I am feeling backed against a wall here, and I am so fucking horny it's bordering on ridiculous.

I could hear Joe and Al talking.

"What the hell is wrong with you?" Joe snapped.

"Not a fucking thing. Let's get a game plan going so we can end this mother fucker."

Shaking my head, I got up and took a shower. When I walked out of the bathroom, the room was eerily quiet. I grabbed some shorts and a t-shirt. I am in desperate need of new clothes. These barely fit me.

I heard a knock on the door. "Hey, Bec, you up?"

"Yeah," I yelled.

Steven came in. He stopped short, looking at the bed then at me. "Bec?"

I closed my eyes. "Yeah, don't worry about it."

"You slept with him? He's your bodyguard."

I laughed. "I'm so fucking horny it's not even funny. I know it's a horrible thing, but you've seen him, right? How could anyone resist him?"

He busted out laughing. "Don't tell Stanly this, but oh my God."

"I know, right. I couldn't help myself."

"Is it true what they say about muscle-bound men?"

I laughed loudly. "It's a fucking myth. Not true." I leaned in on my way by and whispered, "He has the biggest cock I've ever seen." Laughing, I made my way downstairs and into the kitchen. Joe and Al both stopped talking and looked at me.

"Bec," Joe said. "We have a plan to get you out of here. I have a private jet parked at the Napa airport to take you anywhere in the world you want to go." He handed me an envelope. "I put a million dollars in the bank under your new name."

I took the envelope from him, looking past him to Al. He was pissed off. He turned and started to walk out.

"Thank you, Joe, for everything, but I'm not running from him. He murdered my family, and I am going to make him pay for it."

Al spun around. "Like fucking hell you are. You're going to get on that fucking plane, and you aren't looking back."

I laughed. "You aren't the boss of me."

I know, right? Mature.

I think I shocked the hell out of him because he didn't know what to say.

"Joe, I'm not going to run. I've got more money than I can ever spend in my lifetime. If he killed his wife and my family, he is going to pay. I can't keep running. In three months, I am going to have a baby. This needs to end here. It needs to end now."

Al knew I was right. I could see it in his eyes. "No," he said. "No, Bec, you need to leave. Let us deal with him."

I shook my head. "If he thinks I left here, he is going to disappear. As long as he thinks I am here, he will stay around. Find the evidence, find a reason to end him, or I'll give you a reason to put a bullet in his head."

I turned and walked out the back door.

It all happened so fast. I wasn't sure it happened at all, not until I was being dragged across the lawn.

Rick was on the porch. He grabbed my arm and pulled me away from the house.

"You're mine. You need to understand what happened."

"Are you fucking kidding me? Let me go, Rick. I belong to no one."

"You certainly do not belong to that man." He pulled me up to his chest. "Becca, I love you. Come home to the lake house. Marry me," he said, then kissed me.

I kneed him in the balls and took off running when he let me go. I was screaming, all the way up until he tackled me. Yep, the crazy fucker tackled me. Six months pregnant and we landed on my stomach. The pain was immense. He knocked the wind out of me. I felt him get up, lifting me in the air, and then I heard a gunshot. It's all I remember before my body, as well as his, slammed me to the ground again.

I woke up in the hospital, three days ago. My bump is no more. The trauma from the force of the blows of me being slammed into the ground caused a placental abruption. I'm not sure how I feel about that. I mean, it was a baby girl. My bump was a tiny human who didn't do anything but enjoy the little life she had.

I know this might sound cold and unfeeling, but in the end, maybe it's for the best.

I haven't seen Al since I walked out of the house, but Steven told me he shot Rick in the head and then was arrested. It's a huge mess. I'm still at the house on the vineyard. From what I understand, Rick's brother and sister have both been here to see me.

I'm on bed rest for a few more days. I asked Steven to ask them to come back then. I would really like to know what the hell is going on.

I need to sleep. I'm still not sure how I feel about my bump being gone. I'm still pissed off at the both of you, for not caring enough. For seeing me as just a paycheck, when I considered both of you my friend.

Well, Paula, it looks like you might get pretty close to your quota.

CHAPTER FIFTEEN

I'm not sure how many days have passed. Steven brought me food and I ate it. I basically went to the toilet to change myself, and that was it. I haven't showered or anything. I asked them not to bother me, not to turn on the intercom, nothing. I just wanted to be left alone.

I need to get up and make myself presentable, though. I want, no, need to find out what the fuck happened to Rick. So, I dragged myself up, showered, and made my way downstairs. No one was home, but there were messages on the counter for me.

Joe, Alexander, Alice, Paula, and Janet. Nothing from Al. I'm pretty sure I'm not going to ever see him again. Not sure how I feel about that.

I dialed the phone. "Yes, I'd like to speak to Alexander, please."

"I'm sorry, he is unavailable. Can I take a message?"

"Yes, tell him that Becca Hastings returned his call."

"Oh, Miss Hastings, please hold."

I heard his voice, and I just wanted to shove a hot poker down his throat. "Becca, thank you so much for calling me back. I was wondering if Alice and I can come over. We are in Napa and would like to talk to you."

"That's fine."

"Great, we will see you in about twenty minutes." And he hung up the phone.

The man is like the rudest person on the planet. I went to the fridge to grab something cold to drink, then headed out to the front porch to wait for the devil's incarnate. I swear, I don't know what the fuck is wrong with me. I hate him for what he did to my bump. I hate that family for not stopping him from killing my family. My head turns to look at the place my home sat.

I didn't realize I was moving across the lawn as my feet carried me to the place where their lives ended. I don't know what I expected to feel, or what I was thinking. My heart hurt. My whole life had been destroyed because some fucking asshole thought I belonged to him.

I didn't hear the car drive up. I wasn't aware of anything until a hand touched my arm. "Becca," he said softly.

I turned my head to see Alex and Alice standing next to me. "He murdered my family. He burned them to death while they slept in their beds."

I could see the tears in Alice's eyes. "I am so sorry for what he did to you. We didn't know. I promise you, we didn't know."

"How can you say that to me? You knew he was unstable, yet you left me alone with him." My eyes looked at Alice. "You knew I looked like his ex-wife, but you didn't tell me."

"Becca, we are so sorry."

I shook my head. "It doesn't matter anymore. There isn't a fucking thing I can do to change any of it. I didn't ask for this. What do you want?"

"Well, as it turns out, my brother left everything to you."

I just stood there looking at him like he'd shot me. "What?"

"Yes, he changed his will. Everything belongs to you."

"I don't want it. I don't want a fucking thing from him, from you. I don't want it. What happened to Ella?"

I watched as Alice dropped her head. "We found her at the lake house. He just left her there. Becca, he was sick, sicker than we realized. We honestly didn't know he murdered your family. We gave everything we found at the lake house to Joe Blackshaw. It was rather frightening, the information he had acquired on you. We didn't know."

"Just, please, leave me alone. I want nothing from you, from him. I don't ever want to hear your name or his name again. Where is Ella now?"

"Joe Blackshaw has her. We didn't know if you wanted her." Alex nodded, and they turned and started to walk away, but then Alex turned. "We dropped all the charges against Al Blackshaw. We didn't know any of this until a few days ago."

I watched them pull away, and I sank to my knees. He killed my family. My heart was broken, and I mean truly broken.

Broken for the loss of my family.

Broken for my children.

Broken for my husband.

Broken for my Border Collie friend.

Broken for the loss of my bump.

I am broken, unequivocally broken.

I laid down on the grass and seriously prayed for lightning, just like I had prayed for the imaginary lake monster.

What is left in this life for me? I know my life, but who am I to have survived all of this loss?

I believe I am regressing into the state of mind I was in when I moved to the lake house. I just don't want to be anymore.

I'm not sure how long I laid in the sun, on the grass that once was my home. What once was a home filled with love and laughter is now just an empty field, that I am sure one day will grow grapes again.

But in my mind, in my heart, it will always be the place I *was*. The place I *was* a wife. The place I *was* a mother. The place I *was* someone important. The place I *was* alive. The place I just *was*.

The days have passed, and I am still nothing. My poor little ball of fluff doesn't know what to make of all of this. I need to get up and move forward. It's time I take back what is left of my life. I have all this money, and I've never really been anywhere. I think I'll get my passport and travel the world. Maybe I'll just buy another lake house and live my life with my ball of fluff and learn to like myself again. Learn to be me again.

～

Today, I decided to pack my bags and my little ball of fluff and hit the road. If I stay here any longer, I'm afraid I'm going to allow the darkness to swallow me up. I've been here for five weeks now. The doctor gave me a clean bill of health, so it's time to move forward. To where, I haven't a clue. Maybe I'll go back to San Francisco, maybe not. Don't they say you can't go back? Going there would be going back. I'm not that woman anymore.

To be honest, I don't know who the hell I am. Basically, I am nothing. I am no one.

When I came down from my secret room, Steven and Stanly were at the kitchen table.

"I want to say thank you to both of you, for everything you've done to help me, but it's time for me to move on. I can't stay here anymore."

Stanly stood up and hugged me. "I understand, Bec. Know that you are welcome here anytime. If you find yourself lost again, come home. The room is yours, always."

"Thank you, but I think it's time I figure out this life without them."

Steven was crying. "Aww, beautiful, you don't have to be alone. We are here, no matter what." He hugged me tight.

"I know, and I love you both, but it's time for me and my ball of fluff to find our own way. It's just us now."

They helped me put my stuff in my car. We hugged some more, and then I left. I pulled over and got out of the car where our home used to be.

"Goodbye, my loves. You will forever be in my heart. Thank you, Johnathan, for loving me, for giving me the wonderful life we shared. I'm so sorry for what he did to you. I will love you always."

That was it. I got in the car and made my way to L.A.. I needed to see Joe. I needed to know the rest of the story, so I could put it all to rest and move on. I pulled up in the employee parking lot, grabbed my ball of fluff, and headed into the offices.

There was a very pretty, perky blonde at the desk.

"Can I help you?"

I smiled at her. "I'm looking for Joe."

"He's in a meeting. If you want to wait, he shouldn't be much longer."

"Thank you." I sat down, putting Sweetie's crate on the floor."

She was a good kitten, didn't mind driving in the car or being in her crate. I couldn't help but feel bad for her. It's hotel living for us for a while, until I can figure out what to do.

"Can I ask who you are?" the perky blonde asked.

I smiled. "Just tell him Bec is here."

She nodded and picked up the phone. I swear, it was two seconds later and he was walking toward me. I stood up, and he wrapped me in his arms.

"My God, you're a sight for sore eyes."

I laughed. He picked up the crate, and we headed back to his office.

"I don't want to be disturbed," he said to the perky blonde.

She kind of gave me a little bit of a dirty look. Oh well, her problem. Once in his office, he shut the door, put the crate on the floor, and sat down on the couch, pulling me with him.

"What are you doing here?"

"I'm moving forward, but before I can do that, I need to know the rest. I need to know what his family gave you, what all happened. I've said goodbye to John and the kids. I can't go back there. I could feel the darkness pulling me back, and I know John wouldn't want that. Besides, it was the darkness that got me into this mess."

"No, Bec, it wasn't. It was a sick and mentally disturbed man who stalked you, hunted you, and then murdered your family so he could have you. I'm sorry about the baby."

"I'm not. I mean, I am, but I'm not. It was meant to end this way."

He got up and walked over to the desk, picking up a file. "This is what I have. His family took pictures, and the F.B.I. did a thorough investigation. Bec, it's beyond creepy. He had a room in that lake house filled with your life. The kids, John… Fuck he had pictures of the inside of your house. He took his time doing this."

He handed me the file. With shaky hands, I took it from him. Slowly, I opened it and started reading. For years, he watched me. There were detailed notes on how he burned my house down with my family sleeping. He waited for the fires. They come every year, but never had they reached Napa like that. He was the cause. So fucked up.

"I'll leave you to read it all. I'll be right outside."

I just nodded as I turned page after page. There were so many pictures of me. He really was sick. His medical files read like a scary novel. It all started at age ten. He snapped and tried to kill a teacher at the school. God, these people, what they did to their children. There were reports about the school they went to. There was reported abuse, with no findings.

For over an hour, I sat in his office. I hadn't realized I was crying. I felt bad for him, for his brother and sister. For all those children. No one should live like that. In the end, he just wanted to be loved.

When I finished, I put the file on his desk, washed my face, grabbed my ball of fluff, and walked out. I could hear him talking to someone in the room across the hall, so I knocked on the door. It flew open, and standing in front of me was Al.

"Bec? Oh my God." And I was in his arms. I didn't embrace him. I couldn't; I was numb.

When he let me go, I stepped back. Looking at Joe, I whispered, "Thank you." Turning, I walked out. I needed to be alone.

Joe followed me out. "Hey." He turned me around, and I collapsed into his arms. "Oh God, beautiful. I'm so sorry."

I just cried. "I need to go," I managed to say.

"No, let me take you home. You can stay at my place until you get a grip."

I nodded and handed him my keys. He put me and my ball of fluff in the car, and twenty minutes later, he was helping me into his apartment. "Come on." He led me down a hallway to a bedroom, and then to the bed, pulled my shoes off, and laid me down. "Let it go, Bec. I'll be in the living room."

I heard him open the crate, and he handed Sweetie to me. He kissed me on the forehead and then left.

I guess I fell asleep, because when I woke up, all my things were in this room, and here I am sitting in the dark, writing. Sixty-seven thousand words, Paula. I don't think you are going to get your seventy-five thousand. But you will get these.

The horrible story of what was my life for three years. How one woman tried to recover from the devastating loss of her family, but the fucking cosmic universe needed to make sure she suffered immensely before she was given half the chance to make a life for herself.

I have nothing.

I am nothing.

The darkness is calling me, and let me just say, it's sounding more and more like my favorite song.

I suppose I should go show my face and force myself to talk about this shit. I don't think I am ever going to be able to bury it all in my mind. If I hadn't lived it, I wouldn't believe this shit. Not in a million years would I believe a story such as this. But I did live it. I survived it all. At the greatest expense known to man, I fucking survived it.

I walked out of the bedroom and into the living room. Joe was sitting on the couch watching television. He looked at me.

"Feel better?"

"I'm not sure I'm ever going to feel better. Knowing the truth isn't always the healthiest thing."

He chuckled. "I've seen a lot of shit doing this job, but to be honest with you, Bec, this one is the topper. I cannot express to you how sorry I am this happened. John was one of my best friends, and to think that fucker murdered him. Well, you can imagine."

I nodded. "Listen, I'm sorry about this, about being here. If it's all right, I'd like to sleep over. I'll get out of your hair in the morning."

"Bec, you can stay here as long as you want or need."

"I know, but I think it's time I just move forward. I have to get past this. I have to."

He stood up and walked up to me, wrapping me in his arms. "I know. The offer stands, anytime."

"Thanks. Can I get something to eat? Is there a Chinese place around here? I'll buy if you fly."

"I'm buying and flying."

"Whatever. How long? Do you think I have enough time to take a shower?"

He laughed. "About half an hour, and yes. There should be clean towels in the linen closet in the bathroom."

"Thanks. Oh, and just get one of everything on the menu."

He laughed. "Yeah, I remember that about you. I'll see you when I get back."

I made my way back to the room he put me in and shut the door. I just wanted to wash it all away. I wasn't sure it would work, but I just needed to try.

Not sure how long I was in there, but damn if the man's hot water heater wasn't huge. I chuckled to myself as I walked out into the bedroom. I dropped my towel and grabbed my panties, pulling them up. I bent down to grab a pair of shorts when the bedroom door opened. I froze.

Closing my eyes, I knew it wasn't Joe. He would have knocked.

"What the fuck?" I heard.

Shaking my head, I continued to get dressed. I was reaching for my bra when he pulled me against his chest.

"What are you doing here?"

"I was getting dressed, if you don't mind."

"Tell me you didn't fuck my brother."

What the fuck? Did he just say that to me? I mean, really. I struggled to get away from him, but he wouldn't let me go.

"No. Answer the question, Bec."

"You're serious? Fuck you!" I yelled. "Let me go."

"Answer the question."

"What if I did? It doesn't matter what I do. You…" I couldn't even say it. I couldn't say he left me because that would mean it mattered, that he mattered, and I can't do this again.

"I what, Bec?"

"Nothing, just please, let me go. I'm leaving in the morning, so it doesn't matter. None of it matters."

"It matters to me. Did you fuck my brother?"

I wanted to tell him yes, but I'm not a mean person. I couldn't hurt him like that. "Why would you ask me that?"

"I don't know, because you walk out of a shower in my brother's house. He hasn't answered the phone in six hours. Answer me."

"Why does it matter to you what I do, or who I do it with?"

He fucking spun me around and grabbed my face with both his hands. He freaked me out a little. His mouth covered mine. God, what the fuck? Pulling back after I was left stupid and speechless, he looked me in the eyes.

"It fucking matters to me. You matter to me. Bec, tell me you didn't fuck my brother."

I pulled my lip between my teeth and shook my head.

He let out his breath. "God, beautiful, I've been going crazy worrying about you."

I pushed on his chest. "If you were so fucking worried, then why didn't you come back for me. Why did you just leave me there?"

"Because I was in jail for killing that fucker. I just got out about a week ago, and I knew you needed to heal. You needed to bury the ghosts. I couldn't do it for you, and me being there wouldn't have helped you. I was giving you one more week, and I was coming. I gave Joe my notice. I quit my job. That's what you walked in on today."

I was putting my t-shirt on. "Why the hell would you quit your job?"

He stood there looking at me for the longest time. "Don't you know?"

I shook my head, because I didn't have a fucking clue what he was talking about.

"You," was all he said before he was on me again, kissing me, holding me. "Let me in, Bec." His mouth covered mine again. Hell, I couldn't talk if I wanted to. He pulled back again. "Let me in."

"I don't know if I can," I said, on the verge of tears.

"I'll wait. I want you. I want to try with you. I want it all with you."

"Why? We hardly know each other."

"I would rather fight with you than anything else. From the moment I saw you, I felt you. I've never done this before. I've never crossed the line. With you, the line disappeared that day in Stanly's kitchen. I know you felt it, too."

"I did, but I was under duress. My whole world was coming to an end. What we shared was just an extension of that ending."

"You don't believe that, not any more than I do. Take a chance with me."

I stood there looking at him. He was one fine looking man. "But I make mistake after mistake."

"What we shared was not a mistake. You know that. Feel it, Bec. Let yourself feel it. Let me in."

"I... I..."

His fingers trailed along my jaw. "Let yourself feel. Let me in."

What neither of us knew was that Joe was standing in the doorway listening to us. He had a feeling that I was the reason Al quit. He was happy for us, happy knowing that Al would never hurt me, that he would love me for the rest of my life. I didn't know that, though. I wasn't sure I could do it.

I nodded. What the hell, right? What the fucking hell.

He grabbed me and kissed me, then picking me up, he laid us on the bed. We didn't make love, and we didn't fuck. We just kissed. Joe pulled the door closed and left us alone.

∼

Okay, he finally let me get up. I was starving, not to mention, I felt like a teenager walking into the living room. Joe just sat there looking at us. He didn't look happy at all.

"I'm sorry, brother," Al said to him.

Joe just sat there looking at him and then me. He was one of Johnathan's best friends. I was prepared for him to explode. I was even prepared to defend Al. Yeah, I know, I'm a slut. But you know what? I don't care.

Joe stood up and walked over, pulling me into a hug. "I'm not mad. A bit shocked but definitely not mad." Pulling away, he looked at me. "He's a good man, one of the best. For him to quit his job, I know he is serious about you. I know John would approve." Looking at Al, he said, "I've never known you to cross the line. I can't say I'm happy about that, but I know this woman, and I know she is worth it. Hell, if I'm being honest here, if John wasn't one of my best friends, I would have struggled with myself. Take care of her, and don't fucking hurt her, Al."

Al smiled at him, then looked at me. "Not a chance in hell of that happening."

"Good, now, can we eat? I'm starving." Joe laughed, slapping his brother on the back.

We ate, and then my ball of fluff and I left Joe's and came here to Al's a few blocks away. He lives in a really nice place, a place I wouldn't have expected him to live at.

When we walked in, I was brought to my knees when my Border Collie friend ran up to greet me. She knocked me down, licking my face. The tears just came.

"Oh my God. Hi, beautiful," I cried.

I looked at Al, and he smiled. "I wanted you to have her."

"Thank you."

I'm sitting here on the bed while he takes a shower. I so want to fuck this man, but I can't for another few weeks. I need to get another shot. Maybe I'll check in and see about one of those implants. Might be a good idea. I don't think I want to give motherhood a try again, not yet anyway. Besides, I think I'm too old for that. In fact, I have no idea how old Al is. I wonder who is the older brother.

Ella and Sweetie have become fast friends. They share the bed Al got Ella.

My heart is full.

I just happened to look up, and he is leaning against the door frame, looking at me.

"What?" I asked him.

"I didn't think I would ever see you in my bed. I've never had a woman in my bed before."

I laughed. "You, Mr. Stud muffin, have never had a woman in your bed? I find that hard to believe."

He stalked over to me, climbing on the bed in his little towel, and took the computer away. "Believe it. You are the first, and you will be the last."

"Al, before we move any further, I don't want any more children. Are you all right with that?"

"For now." He pulled me into a kiss. "For now," he whispered.

God, the man kissed me stupid.

CHAPTER SIXTEEN

We spent a week at his house learning about one another. It was one of the hardest weeks of my life. No sex. Trust me, when you are basically living with a Norse God, it's really a very difficult thing to do. But doctor's orders. He is so sweet, not letting me touch him.

"If you can't enjoy pleasure, then I can't," he said.

I had to laugh. "What if giving you pleasure brings me pleasure?"

Laughing, he pulled me into his arms. "Nice try, but when the doctor says you are good to go, trust me, you are going to be sore for a very long time."

Admittingly, I swallowed hard.

So, I went to the doctor's. I got my okay, and I had an implant put in my arm. I'm not taking a chance on an accidental bump.

We are coming off our week in bed, and he was right. I am sore as fuck. Honestly, I am sitting here smiling at how ironic that sounds.

We are taking off in the morning, on a driving trip across the country, so I'm not sure this machine is going to get much use. But that's okay.

I believe now that I am healed. I believe that everything that happened with Rick brought me here to Al, to this life I am about to embark on. This man is loving, caring, and as gentle as a kitten. Oh yeah, and our little ball of fluff and Ella are coming along for the ride. For the time being, they are our children.

For now, I am signing off.

Thank you, Paula, for being in my head and making me a responsible person, a responsible writer, meeting your quota.

Janet, I'm not sure what to say to you. I could blame you for all of this, for dragging me out into the public, and for putting me on that stage. That stage is where he saw me, where he began his hunt. That stage ultimately destroyed my life.

But, and there is always a but in situations like this, if none of this had happened, I wouldn't have found him, and in the end, I believe I was supposed to.

So, from Within the Ashes of destruction, I found life. I found me. I found him.

Paula,

It took a very long time for me to write this manuscript, and I wasn't even sure that I was ever going to publish it, but, and there is always a but in situations such as this, I think that it should be read.

You were always my choice to publish it, and I am glad that Alexander kept his word, concerning your future. Although, at the time I made the deal, I had no clue how deep into it all of you were.

I know now that no one but the Railing family had any clue what was going on, so I can't blame you. I can't hold it against you.

I would like to believe that, at one point, we were friends, but somewhere deep inside of me, I know we weren't. It's all right. I'm okay now.

Al and I spent a year on the road, living life. I'm married now, to him, to the Norse God, who never lets me forget who I am.

We have a lovely little beach house on a lake that I am praying doesn't have a lake monster in it.

I'm in love, happy, and finally at peace.

Please, promise me that you will not change a thing in this manuscript if you so choose to publish it. It doesn't matter either way to me. It was my salvation, my pathetic way of clinging to life when I was sure the darkness was going to win.

The darkness comes every now and again, but Al makes sure to fill me with light.

Again, thank you for everything you did in making my life a living hell, and I say that with kindness, because if you hadn't, I wouldn't have this life I have now, with this man who loves only me; well, and our little ball of fluff, who is now a giant ball of fluff, along with my beautiful Border Collie, Ella, who was ultimately the beginning of the light at the end of the tunnel of darkness I existed in.

Have a good life, Paula, because I am.

Always,

Becca Storm

More Books by Cin Medley

Broken
One Hundred Acres
Is this Life
Six Months
Lyssa's Journey
Winter Harbor
Beautiful Liar
Justice
Secrets
Lines Crossed
Everything She Thought

www.ingramcontent.com/pod-product-compliance
Lightning Source LLC
Chambersburg PA
CBHW020410210626
46816CB00006BB/2211